Daniell

My lovely ☺ I wish
you all the best. Hate
you for leaving... but love
you for the support hun!
I'll missssss you a lot!
Keep in touch xoxo

Yalesa.W
Apr. 10. 2010
xoxo

you better *love* it !

Something Special

JALESA WALLACE

authorHOUSE®

AuthorHouse™
1663 Liberty Drive
Bloomington, IN 47403
www.authorhouse.com
Phone: 1-800-839-8640

First published by AuthorHouse 2/12/2010

ISBN: 978-1-4490-6967-4 (e)
ISBN: 978-1-4490-6969-8 (sc)
ISBN: 978-1-4490-6970-4 (hc)

Library of Congress Control Number: 2010900510

Printed in the United States of America
Bloomington, Indiana

This book is printed on acid-free paper.

Dedicated to NKJ my "Something Special"
& Madame, Love You

CHAPTER 1

Working Hard

As Nathan knelt on bended knee; he looked up at his girlfriend, Angelique. She stood bright eyed, excited for what her heart knew was coming next. "You're my best friend, my heart and my everything in life that matters."

Jumping and moving her body around as if she needed to urinate, Angelique could barely contain her stance. "Marry me."

Angelique hopped on the bench to reach her boyfriends height; jumped on him, wrapped her legs around his waist and kissed him all over his face. Nathan laughed, seeing his girlfriend so elated. "Is that a yes?"

She stopped slobbering on his face and smiled very peacefully, "Yes sweetie I'll marry you, in a heart beat."

Nathan and Angelique were inseparable, for the past two years. As he finished law school and she got her business degree, they were never apart. They met at a Deli Shop two years ago that day and it was Angelique who approached Nathan.

"This line is mad long." Nathan turned around and realized this chocolate angel.

"Tell me about it, I been here for about 15 minutes."

She chuckled, "So why you still here, your girlfriend doesn't pack your lunch?"

He bashfully looked away, realizing she was trying to pick him up. "My girlfriend didn't pack my lunch. And if I had one, she would tell me that the sandwiches here are much better."

She nodded and stuck out her hand, "Angelique Walters."

He laughed, "Nathan Walker." She looked at him wondering why he laughed before responding. "I'm sorry, you just sounded real professional, like a business woman answering her cell phone or something."

She smiled at him as he blushed in his defense, "I'm a business major at Stony Brook University."

"That's impressive; I'm in East York Law School, finishing my final year." He told her.

After half an hour of talking and finally getting their sandwich, he asked her for her number. "You live on campus?"

"Yes I do."

"What's the number to your dorm?"

She pulled her coat over her shoulder and answered in the most serious tone, "Room 166."

Nathan looked at her shocked. "I meant your phone number."

Picking up her purse she smiled, "I know you did." Angelique Walters walked out the deli door with her sandwich and Nathan watched this aggressive but yet civil, open minded individual grace him with her presence, as she invited herself into his life. He'd be a fool if he didn't call.

Nathan rolled over on his side to see the spot beside him empty. "Angel!" He hollered out to his fiancée, Angelique. They had been engaged for merely 12 hours and still, it seemed like forever. Nathan and Angelique had been together for two years since that afternoon in the Deli Store. They completed each other and it was hard to remember a time in their life where they were happier. Yes they did have arguments and normal relationship disagreements. But which relationship didn't? So, they got engaged.

"Babe, have you seen my berry?"

Nathan squinted and smiled out loud, "Don't worry babe, I'm sure you'll get a text message or a page soon enough and you'll be able to locate it." He spoke too soon, within 10 seconds her phone went off, "New Message from Michael." Nathan was suddenly alert. "Who's Michael?"

"My new boss I was telling you about babe."

Nathan leaned over and reached for the pearl. He read aloud, "Good Morning Sunshine! Does he always call you sunshine?"

Angelique walked stressfully back into the bedroom. She grabbed the blackberry out of his hand. "Yes!"

Nathan laughed, "Wow, Why? You're more like a thunder storm to me." She kissed him and just stared into his deep brown eyes.

"I love you."

"I love you too sunshine." She picked up her luggage and blew a kiss to her fiancé. "What no breakfast?" He asked.

Her phone rang, "Angelique Walters, talk to me." As she walked out the door, she moved the phone from her ear, "Breakfast is on the stove, I love you, and I can't wait to get back so I can marry you." She closed the front door and he yelled "I'LL MISS YOU!" He laid there in silence until his phone went off. It was a text message from Angelique, "I already do." He closed the message and stared at his cell phone background, it was picture of him and Angelique. "What am I gonna do without you for two months, Angel?"

He sighed miserably and headed towards the shower. As the water slapped against his caramel skin he ran his hands through his tight curly hair and stressed about the day he had ahead of him. He envisioned his wedding day, and could see how pretty and expensive it was going to be; after all he was marrying Hilary Banks. That factor aside, it was a good vision. This girl was his left and his right and there was no doubt in his mind that Angelique would be the one he waited for. As he dried himself off, his house phone rang, it was his mother. "Hi mom."

"Hi. How are things going Nate?" His mother asked.

"Well, my girlfriend has left for a business trip, I have an eight hour shift ahead of me, I'm defending a minor on sexual assault charges and I have a heavenly dinner with my parents tonight. How could it be any better?"

Evelyn Walker laughed at her sons' humor. "I love you too Nate. Thanks for coming over tonight though. Since I've been on my vacation, I swear your dad is bored of me by now. He needs to see his son. Get some boy time in, you know?"

His dad was always a family man, putting his wife above all, but he always pushed things aside for his son, just as Nathan pushed *them* aside for Angelique. Nathan shoved the remainder of his English muffin in his mouth, and quickly rushed his mom off the phone. "I'm sure he's not bored of you, but mom I got to run, I'll see you tonight."

As Nathan's BMW pulled into the lot of the Wilson Law Firm that he worked for, he noticed Angelique's make up purse in his glove compartment. As he opened it to put his gloves in there, he looked through it and took note of it's contents. He zipped it back up and sighed. His phone went off and it was another text message from Angelique, "Baby, you'll be okay." Nathan smiled to himself, picked up his brief case and set the alarm on his car.

He walked into his office as his secretary listed off a list of important messages for him. "Thanks Victoria, just leave it in my mailbox please, I'll take care of it when I'm done with today's trial."

Victoria nodded, "Yes sir."

When Nathan finally sat down at his desk before leaving for the courtroom, he looked over his notes and made sure the points he had were legit. He was determined to prove his client innocent beyond a reasonable doubt, forget guilty, because that, his client was definitely not. He could go on for hours to the judge and jury why his client was innocent. He could also go on for hours as to why his client had been given poor treatment. But Nathan was a lot smarter than Judge Jameson gave him credit for. Because Nathan excelled six months after he joined the Wilson firm, judges felt like he was given special treatment, for whatever reason. That wasn't the case, he was just damn good at his job, and because he was young, they envied him and all his accomplishments even more. But Nathan didn't mind, haters were good, they were a boost of confidence and they made the satisfaction of winning all his cases even better.

Walking into the courtroom, Nathan smiled as he rose and Judge Jameson entered his seat. "Morning counselors." Judge Jameson eyed Nathan and saw him smiling.

"You mean GOOD morning." Nathan replied.

The prosecution team laughed, having no idea why Nathan said it with such a realm of certainty surrounding him and his table. He was going to win that case. Nathan knew it, his client knew it and Judge Jameson knew it. It's just too bad the prosecution team, didn't.

CHAPTER TWO

Over Before It Has Begun

It seemed as if the trial would never ever end. From his 9:00am start, it was now eight thirty at night. Judge Jameson was really a pain in the ass. Besides, what the hell would this judge know; he never had kids and was just bitter about children because his wife wouldn't have kids with him, and still left him and had children with another man. Yes, he heard it through the courtroom grapevine. And Judge Jameson made it clear that he despised Nathan for when he started out, he was merely a child himself.

He drove over to his parents house and just sat in the drive way. As much as he hated to declare it, he hated visiting his parents alone. Angelique or his older sister Tanya would always go with him. Ever since he went away to Law School and graduated with honorable marks, his visits with his parents had become limited. Once he started his career, he was always busy with work or Angelique. And his parents blamed Angelique for that new found bad habit in their son. But he was his own man. He had his own car, his own house, his now fiancé and a well paying career as a lawyer. So why did he feel as though he was missing something, something special?

He shut his car door and walked up the seven steps to his parents' house. Every time he walked up those steps he remembered hanging out with his friends; Steven, Gregory and Shawn. They all remained friends throughout high school, university and the different endeavors they all went through. Unlike girls, they let nothing come between them.

"Hi baby." Evelyn hugged and kissed her son.

"Hey mom, how are you?"

"Good sweetie, good. I thought you weren't going to show." He could see how much his mom missed his company. They walked into the kitchen and he looked at his dad.

"Hey dad." The biggest smile appeared on his dads face.

"Is that my son? With such a shocking resemblance of me, of course it is. How long has it been Nate, 3, 4 months?" Nathan smiled, ashamed, hugged his dad and sat down beside him on the available stool. "How was your day Nate?"

"My day. What to say about that. I was defending a minor on sexual assault charges and it just dragged on for 4 and a half hours. But we made it out alive. And better yet, on top."

His mom just looked at him and smiled. "I'm very proud of you Nathan."

His dad, Jeffery Walker looked over at her, "We're very proud of you Nathan." Nathan nodded a stressful nod and said, "Thank you guys, I'm proud of me too."

Evelyn laughed, "So, Nathan what's new honey? You're GLOWING."

Nathan laughed and avoided all eye contact.

"Yeah Nathan, did something happen between you and Angelique?" His father asked, unsure why, he did.

"Yeah, we're engaged."

It was as if the walls in the house were moving in closer and closer and there was no way out. It just slipped out of his mouth. Nathan was always a little hesitant when it came to Angelique around his father, who thought Angelique was no good for his son, from day one. And Nathan never ever understood why. Nathan looked at his mother who wanted to speak but knew her husband would scold her if she had.

You could cut the tension in the room three ways and share it among the Walker family. Finally, Nathan spoke "Last night, we decided to get engaged." He looked at the disgust on his dads face. "I love her dad." Again, it was silent for another minute and a half. With pleading eyes Nathan looked over at his mother for support, knowing well enough that she couldn't give any.

"I'm happy for you and Angelique, Nathan. This is so exciting baby. Congratulations." She exclaimed hugging her last child. "So have you two picked a date as yet?"

Looking at his dad Nathan shook his head no. "She headed out for a business trip this morning, so we didn't get a chance to do that as yet."

That pissed his dad off. "So you're going to sit here and condone this marriage Evelyn?"

"Yes because he's my son, I love him and whatever decisions he makes, I'll forever be here behind him."

Nathan looked at his father after letting go of his mother. "Dad, I didn't come here, asking for your blessing, because I don't need it. And what do you have against my fiancé anyways?"

The fire in his eyes was as clear as day, but Nathan glared right back with as much fire if not more. "You're young Nathan and..."

"YOUNG? I'm damn near THIRTY dad. Stop playing games, what's the real reason why you have a problem with Angelique, because I'm not buying the '*you're too young shit.*' I'm a lawyer dad; I'm trained to break down liars. Now spill it."

His dad looked at him and just started to laugh, "Get out of my house with your fancy law degree Nathan. We put our asses on the line for you so YOU can live the lavish lifestyle you live now and for what, so you can throw it away on a girl who could care less about you and your well being. Answer me this, how much money did Angelique put into that mansion you're living in?"

Evelyn jumped in, "Now Jeff calm down, I think you've gone a bit too far."

He stepped to his wife and said, "You don't know how far I could go."

Fear had glazed over her eyes and torture glazed over his. "Stop it Jeffery, you're scaring me."

Nathan pulled his mother aside, trying very calmly to keep his cool he said "mom can we talk in the other room please?"

She looked at her husband and looked back at Nathan, "Yes Baby, let me fix you a plate first."

Nathan nodded and turned his back towards his dad.

"Nate." He turned around. "You've disappointed me in the recent decision you've made son."

"Son? That would only mean you would have to be my father. But fathers don't say any of what you've just said about me and MY FUTURE! Fuck how you feel, it's not about you Jeff!"

His dad laughed hysterically, joker from Batman hysterically and lit a cigarette. Nathan couldn't figure out why he laughed or why he smoked a cigarette, his dad never smoked. Staring at his dad he could see, his hand shaking as he brought the cigarette to his lips. He walked out of the kitchen confused and then turned back.

"You're disappointed in me? I'm disappointed in you, Dad." The look on his dads face turned from devilish monster, to sad puppy. It looked as though, with that one line he had hurt his dads' feelings. But he didn't care.

Nathan walked into his old bedroom and threw himself on a sofa his mom moved in there when he turned 18. He looked again on his cell phone background at the love of his life and shook his head, "Why don't they see what I see?" Evelyn walked into her sons' room and flung herself on his bed. "It's in the microwave babe." Nathan nodded and closed his eyes, just thinking about everything that just occurred. He looked at his mom just staring at him, knowing she had so much to say but couldn't say it. "Since when did dad start smoking?" She looked as though she felt bad. "I'm sorry you had to see that Nathan, I tried to talk him out of it but it's a bad habit he picked up a couple months ago."

"What's the matter with him?" She sat up straight.

"You've noticed?"

"Of course I've noticed mom, he's smoking and he just stares at me like he doesn't even know me, and he shakes and..."

She cut him off, "He wouldn't like to know that we're back here talking about him Nathan. Come on you know your father better than that Nate."

"Do I mom? Is he the same guy, because MY dad doesn't smoke! My dad doesn't make vicious attacks at my fiancé. What's that about?" Evelyn's son had caught her in an awkward moment and she didn't know how to protect and defend her husband while staying true to her son. "I can't explain it to you right now Nathan. Now is not the time, okay? I love you and your dad loves you and I promise I will explain it to you when the time is right, just please..." Her eyes welted up in tears. "Please just don't say anything to upset him." Nathan sat up in his seat and was worried. "Why are you crying mom? Did I upset you, I'm sorry." Through her tears she shook her head no and smiled "Just remember what I said." And she walked out of the room.

He knew even though his mom took his side, she felt the same way about Angelique that his father did. But his mother never would express that with words or even through her behavior. She loved her son and if he was happy, she was in and externally happy as well. He sighed a loud sigh and further stressed on what just happened with him and his dad. It was stupid and Nathan knew that, he just couldn't figure out what the problem was with him and Angelique. They had a few verbal attacks; but Nathan reassured the two of them that when it came to each other and him, they were not allowed to comment. And that's the way it remained. Jeffery never interfered with his sons' relationship because he respected his sons' wishes. And still, Nathan was itching to know, what the big problem was, because it was obvious that there was one.

After a very loud roaring in his stomach, Nathan noticed his mother hadn't made her way out of the kitchen. With that, he heard a plate crash to the floor and his mother scream. He ran out to see what was happening. To his surprise, there was his father with a gun to his mothers head, as she cried and strained to break free.

Nathan walked over closer and she begged, "Nathan please stay where you are baby, please!" He listened to her and everything just ran through his head at that time that he could hardly speak.

"I didn't mean to disappoint you dad. Just let her go."

"NO son, I didn't mean to disappoint you."

Nathan couldn't wrap his mind around, why his dad was acting the way he was. "I need you to put the gun down."

"Why Nathan? Because you'd be too embarrassed to defend your dad on first degree murder. OH, my bad, you don't defend people like me only the rich people who pay the big bucks who have made you the snot nose punk of a man you claim to be."

It was extremely hard for Nathan to keep his cool; he wanted to say some things to his father, but as his mother desperately shook her head and pleaded with her eyes for him not to respond back, he knew he couldn't.

"I know I neglected our relationship together."

His dad cut him off, "SHUT UP! SHUT UP! YOU SHUT ME AND YOUR MOTHER OUT OF YOUR LIFE. AND LET YOUR LITTLE ANGEL TAKE OVER YOUR LIFE AND ERASE US OUT OF IT. ARE YOU BLIND?"

Nathan began to tear up and his blood felt as though it was cold as ice. "Some lawyer you are! I thought you were trained to break down liars. Not doing such a good job with that now are you?" His dad mocked.

"I can fix this, I can fix us. Dad just put the gun down."

Jeff shook his head no and tears ran down his face. "YOU CAN'T YOU CAN'T FIX ME! IT'S TOO LATE."

Confused by what his dad said, Nathan held onto the banister by the front door to regain his stance and come to some sort of understanding.

He saw nothing but fear through all his mothers' tears in her eyes. But the most fear was in his fathers' eyes. He didn't know what he was doing; he didn't want to do it. He wasn't that kind of man. "This isn't you dad. Don't do this to us or yourself."

"Like what you're doing to us?"

With that he fired the gun off in his wife's head and she fell to the wooden floor, blood pouring out like crazy. "ARE YOU OUT OF YOUR FUCKING MIND!?" Nathan hollered as he reached for his phone.

His dad looked at him, "I think I am."

And in an instant, ended his life, with the same gun, and the same shot to the head.

He ran over to his parents and laid there with them and cried and cried. Covered in blood he took out his phone and through his tears and pain and anger he said, "there's an emergency at 67 Lancaster Drive, my parents are dead and…' he broke off. 'I'm afraid if you don't hurry up, I'll kill myself too."

The police showed up in about 6 minutes and Nathan was a mess. As they beat down the front and side doors, Nathan couldn't move. He couldn't even answer when an officer asked if anyone was in there. Lucky for him and the officers, the door was easy to break down. Nathan shot his head up as they entered with guns in the air.

"What happened here?" An officer asked him.

Still fighting to see through his tears Nathan's knees shook as he tried to stand.

"Are you hurt?" Another officer asked, as the ambulance came bursting in.

He managed to say, "I'm good, it's my mom and…m m m-my dad who need your help."

The ambulance had Nathan sit down on the couch and covered his shoulders with a blanket as he trembled at the site of such a massacre. Nathan looked as the ambulance checked for heart beats and whatever else they were doing. Nathan couldn't come to terms with what was being done; he just wanted to know that his parents were going to make it.

Officers split up to see if anyone else was home, while another sat in the couch across from Nathan. "What happened?"

With his head in his hands, Nathan looked up at the officer, "There was an argument, and uh, uh my dad uh, he shot my mom in her head." Reliving the moment Nathan was devastated that he had to think about again, so soon. But it was all he could think about. The officer didn't show any emotion.

"Where is your father now?"

Nathan looked at her as if she should have already known. "Laying right there on the floor beside my mom."

She straightened her posture, almost as if she felt uncomfortable. "That's your dad?" Nathan nodded and looked over to see the ambulance load and strap his parents on a stretcher.

"He killed himself?"

Nathan looked at her as if she was trying to accuse him of something. "Yes he did. Do you want me to show you the footage I recorded?"

He stood up, disgusted and walked over to the paramedics. "Please tell me it's not too late and there is something you can do."

As they wheeled his parents outside, one responded, "What do you do for a living?"

"I'm a lawyer." Nathan answered wondering what the hell that had to do with anything.

"That's good because unfortunately you have two funerals on your hands. Sorry for your loss."

Heartless. Even their "Sorry for your loss" meant nothing. As the paramedics drove off, a few officers instructed Nathan on his next steps for he had no clue what would follow.

As tears took over Nathans face he couldn't help but wonder how was he going to tell his sister? How was he going to live without his parents? According to his dad, he was already living without them.

So why did his life feel so much different when there was nothing left of them but their blood in a pool on the living room floor?

CHAPTER THREE

No One To Blame, But Myself

"Nathan Walker, talk to me." Nathan answered his phone two days after his parents' death. "Hey, I'm actually not going to be in the office from today, March the 2nd until I return on the 19th. My assistant Victoria will be keeping track of all my messages and any important details I need to be aware of. Therefore, I shall be up to speed by the trial on the 28th." He hung up and poured himself some coffee. Knowing that he had over two weeks to pull himself together, made the days a little easier to get through. He needed to heal, that was a given, but along with the assistance from his older sister from Atlanta, he had a huge funeral to plan in honor of his parents.

After sitting back down in his king size bed with a fluffy white and grey duvet, he decided to call his fiancé. When she answered she was in the middle of lunch get together with some co -workers.

"Hey baby."

"Hi, Angel. Can we talk?"

"Sure baby I can spare five minutes, how's my baby doing?"

Not knowing how to say it, his words fell out, "I need you to come down here next weekend."

"Why?"

"My parents died."

She paused and gasped. She broke up a little, "What do you mean?"

"Exactly what I said." Nathan struggled to say what he really wanted to say.

"Both of them?"

"Yes." Tears filled Nathans eye lids.

"What happened Nathan, oh my God!"

He shook his head to himself, "Angelique, I would prefer if you could come and be here so I can explain this to you a little better. Over the phone, just isn't doing it. I need you here with me. I can't get through this on my own."

"Baby I love you, and I'm sorry you're going through this alone but I don't understand what happened and how it happened? I need you to explain this to me before I make a decision like this."

"A decision like this? This isn't a blue shirt or green shirt kind of a decision Angelique. This is a life you're dealing with. Mine!"

She was silent.

"Just come Angel, gosh. Is it that hard?" Nathan could hear people calling Angelique's name, rushing her to get back to the conversation with them.

"Nathan, I love you okay, but I booked this meeting three months ago and I can't get out of it. How is it going to look to the company if I don't show?"

"The same way it'll look when you don't show up to the funeral. It's a family emergency, I'm sure they would understand."

She hesitated. "Nathan, trust me when I say they wouldn't."

Nathan couldn't begin to believe what he was hearing. "I have to go." He hung up and wanted to throw his phone across the room, but it vibrated as he was about to. "Yes Angelique."

"What, no I love you?"

"How could I say that to you, so you could lie to me and say it back?"

"What? I do love you Nathan."

"Then you'd be here, when I need some support, some flippin reassurance that everything is going to be okay."

She was silent and then she struggled to say, "They're gone Nathan."

"Not just that, I also meant with me and you Angelique."

"Everything's going to be okay, why wouldn't it be?" She pleaded.

"Are you going to be here?"

She whispered, "Nathan I can't baby. I'm sorry, but I gotta go."

He didn't respond.

"I love you." She forced on him.

He sighed, "I love you too." He shook his head and hung up, "That's why it wouldn't be okay."

Nathan just stared into the ceiling of his bedroom. Not wanting to get up and move on with the funeral arrangements. How could she be so inconsiderate? He didn't want to believe what his dad said that night, but he found it hard to fight with his thoughts. His cell phone rang once again, this time it was his older sister Tanya. "Hey big sis, what's up?"

She sounded happier than she should. That's what Nathan liked about her, no matter what was going on in her life, Tanya could cover it up for someone else, so they wouldn't feel as if crying or hurting was always the answer.

"Hey bro, how you hanging in there?"

Nathan eyed a picture on his dresser of his mom and his dad and placed his hand on his forehead. "I'm hanging on by a thread. But for the life of me, I'm hanging on."

Tanya was proud of her baby brother, not many people could witness something like that and be sane, and he was not only sane but, holding it together. "Good, I'm glad to hear that. Only the strong survive."

Nathan laughed out loud at his sisters comments. His dad always said that when Nathan and Tanya fought when they were younger or when they started their post secondary education. Actually, he said it for everything; something on the news, if they had relationship problems or even just to joke around with them.

"How are you and the family doing?" He asked concerned more so about his niece.

"Well Devon is still in shock, but he's been really supportive. He takes Eve out so she can get her mind off of it. And she really just can't wrap her mind around the idea of it. She constantly wants to call her, because you know mom and dad were suppose to come down here this weekend. So she was looking forward to that."

Nathan nodded to himself. "And yourself?"

Nathan could hear her pause as the tears streamed down her cheek. "I'm sorry."

"No, Nate, don't be. I have my good days and my bad days. And if you can be strong Nathan, we'll be strong together."

He reassured her, "Only the strong survive Tanya."

She laughed. "I actually called you Nate, to let you know my flight comes in tonight at 6:30, terminal 2."

Nathan wrote it down on a piece of paper and listened as Tanya continued to speak. "I'll have my cell on, so I'll be able to tell you exactly where I'm at, for you to pull the limo up out front and pull out the red carpet for me."

Again, laughing at his sisters stupid comment he answered her, "What Devon and Eve aren't coming with you?" Nathan was referring to his brother in law and his niece.

"Not until, Saturday morning, Eve has school remember?"

He forgot. "Yeah, my bad! Alright Tanya, I'm going to order the flowers and stop over at mom and dads work, so I'll see you later on tonight."

"No I don't want you to do both. I'll go to dads work tomorrow morning, okay?"

"Sure thing."

"Oh and Nate, what kind of flowers you getting?"

"NO CLUE!"

They laughed and ended the conversation.

Nathan laid around for another half an hour before he brought himself to get up and leave. He looked at the paper he had rested on his table for the programs. He uploaded the picture of his parents from his dresser onto his PC and watched it quickly appear on his screen.

Just staring at those loving faces, he found it hard to believe how much of a monster his dad was. Yes, his dad was a strict man and had a temper, but he rarely let it loose. Maybe the occasional family failure or argument with his mom, but it wasn't serious enough to murder anyone, or commit suicide! What the hell did Angelique do to make his dad hate her so much? It was beyond Nathan.

He drove down to Rosie's Rosary, where he decided to deal with the flowers considering his sister dealt with the church already.

"Hi, welcome to Rosie's, what's the occasion?" A young girl in about her early twenties questioned.

Nathan drew a blank.

"Wedding, prom, party, gift.."

"Funeral."

Her smile quickly dumbed down and she cleared her throat. "Oh, I'm sorry. What exactly were you looking for? A man or a woman?"

His voice became rather coarse and he barely got out, "both." Throughout the entire time with the young lady he felt, like a weak little boy. "You know what; I think I should come back with my sister."

As soon as the opportunity came up, he left and drove down to his moms work. They needed to learn that his mother wouldn't be returning to work and why. He walked into an elegant building entitled, The Dixon & Green Social Corporation. He walked up to the main desk and asked for the floor in which he would find where his mom worked. The clerk directed him to the fourth floor and he found his moms desk.

He stood there for a minute realizing his mom was the secretary and wouldn't be there to ask him who he was there to see or if he had an appointment.

He walked past her desk to an office with the name Casey Green on the door in bold golden letters. He thought to himself, this must be the Green in Dixon & Green. He knocked on the door and no answer. He looked through the glass and the lights were on, papers were scattered all over the desk and the phone ringing off the hook.

"Yes I know I'm not the neatest when I'm frustrated." He turned and faced a beautiful woman, about 5'5, thick thighs, an ass to kill and long thick silky black hair. She wore her glasses down to the brim of her nose as she blew her breath to cool her coffee.

She stuck out her hand, "Hi, I'm Casey."

He stared at her, "This is your office?"

She smiled at him and again he noticed how white her teeth were, he felt like he was watching a Colgate commercial.

"Yes Sir, come on in. And your name is?"

He sat down and took note of how her high waisted skirt hugged her hips and tightened her belly. How the collar of her shirt just naturally stayed so fresh. "I'm Nathan."

She just stared at him, "You look oddly familiar. Have we met before?"

Nathan laughed, "Nathan Walker."

She put her huge coffee mug down and smiled, "Evelyn's son? Yeah I recognize you from her desktop out front."

He nodded and smiled back at her. Something about her changed the way he was in the Flower Shop. She brought life to him and besides it was a bonus just looking at such a successful black woman.

Trying to organize her papers she asked, "So Nathan, what's going on?" He didn't know whether or not he should just spring it on her or work his way in. He didn't want to set the mood into a happy affair when it wasn't that.

"It was critical that I meet with you, my mothers' employer."

She was smarter than he gave her credit for. ,

"Why does she need more vacation time? Is everything alright Nathan?"

Fiddling with his thumbs and his thoughts he begged for an interruption of a phone call or a client or something. Nothing. Being as strong as he knew how to be he said "On the night of the 29th my mom was murdered."

She clasped her left hand over her mouth and Nathan could see her eyes instantly fill with water. Within a second they ran down her cheeks and she removed her Prada glasses and grabbed some tissues from a near by box.

"Who would do that? She was an amazing woman." She asked, breaking up.

"My dad." Still crying she looked at him like you're joking right? But Nathan continued. "I was there, I seen the whole thing and then he killed himself. And 99% of me blames myself. Why'd I go there that night?"

As she regained her inner strength and wiped away her tears, she held his hand and said, "Don't do this to yourself."

He stood up, 'I have to dammit! They were arguing about me. How I left them and I didn't care about them. And I'm a stuck up rich lawyer who lives this abundant lifestyle that I excluded them from. I did that. I killed them; I did this to myself, my sister, to you."

Casey was quiet. She realized he must have endured a lot that night and needed to vent. He just paced back and fourth in her office and threw himself back in his seat. "How could I let that happen? I had the ability to stop this and here I am, handing out oral funeral invitations."

"It's more complicated than that Nathan, trust me." She looked as though she knew more than she was letting him in on. She was way too confident when she said, trust me.

Her office phone rang and she answered, "Excuse me for a second Nathan. Good afternoon Miss Sanchez, I do realize you have a 5:30 appointment today, I still have you penciled in. And I will see you in an hour, love. Take care." She looked at him, "Sorry about that."

He shook his head, "Don't be. Look I won't take up your time, but the Funeral is March 10th and my sister and I would like it if you would come. I know my mom would have wanted you there."

As he sat back down, she put her glasses back to the brim of her nose, flipped through her planner, ran her index finger down to the tenth and picked up her phone and dialed ten digits. Wiping the remainder of her tears from her face she spoke;

"Hi Mitchell, sorry I didn't reach you and I hate to do this over your voice mail, but something has come up and I won't be able to attend the conference next weekend. Sorry for any inconvenience, but my next available three day weekend is April 6th. Can you please let me know, and I will definitely clear up any misunderstandings with the Glidden Firm. Thanks and again, my apologies. But' she made eye contact with Nathan as he was impressed with her, greatly impressed. 'I have somewhere I need to be.' And she hung up.

"You didn't have to do that."

And still. Through her tears and obvious pain, she smiled and nodded, "Yes I did. I loved your mother like my own mother. And I didn't know your dad personally but I knew him through the stories your mom would tell. And he wasn't a bad man Nathan, he needed help. I still want to pay my respects."

She laughed, "Why you looking at me like that?"

"You're my Angel. I mean, you're like an Angel."

"So tell me what this Angel can do to help."

"Oh wow! I didn't come here with the intentions of asking you to help out. But, I just came back from Rosie's Rosary down on Fairview, and I have no clue what kind of flowers would be nice."

Without a hesitation she identified that his mom should get a mixture of white and pink carnations with red roses and for his dad, deep purple tulips and white carnations in both bouquets and floral arrangements

"I don't even know what carnations look like but I trust you." He said smiling.

"Would you like me to stop by Rosie's and order them myself?"

"Please. That would mean a lot."

Nathan pulled out his cheque book from a leather planner that held all his business information. "How much are we talking, 5...600?"

Running her fingers through her hair she smiled, "I have a cheque book too Nathan. I want to do this, it's not an inconvenience."

"You sure?"

"I'm sure you have more things to deal with this entire week, let me take this stress off your shoulders even if it's a little stressor. And besides, the Green on the front of the building out there doesn't represent the color of the grass or the money we make. It represents me. So trust me when I say I got this."

This girl was too much! "Thank you Casey."

As she finally cleared her desk off and proceeded to write in her planner, she looked up and with the most sincerity and willingness in her eyes she said, "No thank you Mr. Walker. And I'm truly sorry for your loss."

Half way out her door he sighed, "Don't be, every mans loss is another's gain."

Casey watched him as he waited for the elevator to come. As he walked into the elevator, their eyes made four and he waved goodbye. She waved back and opened her wallet sized planner. A tear rolled down her cheek as she penciled in the funeral of her dear friend.

Casey walked into the hall, out to Evelyn's desk and sat in her seat. She moved the mouse to her computer around and looked at her desktop background. It was a picture of Nathan, Tanya, her husband and her herself. They looked happy and unbreakable.

That picture and those smiles showed no signs of pain, or any sort of problems. But Casey knew there were problems. Nathan was right, she knew more than she was telling him. She was close with his mother and knew everything there was to know about why the night of the 29th ended the way it did. If she wasn't certain she had a feeling what the source of it was. No one could prevent that and she was afraid Nathan didn't know that. And he blamed himself.

As the Walker family stared and smiled back at her, she logged off the computer. The screen said, "Goodbye Evelyn", and Casey read it aloud as a single tear ran from her eye,

"Goodbye Evelyn."

CHAPTER FOUR

And Then There Were Two

Monday March 5th, Nathan and his sister had a few things they needed to take care of. The first day she arrived they went over to their parents house to straighten things out. Lucky for them, their parents didn't have a lot of belongings. They organized things that Nathan would keep, Tanya would keep, things they'd put in storage because they simply couldn't part with it, and other things that would obviously end up in the garbage.

After about 4 and half hours of doing that, they called it a night and decided to deal with the insurance companies and all that secretary work another time. Preferably, after the funeral.

They spent the next four days making first and final decisions on things such as, the catering company, the songs of choice, the program and most importantly the guest that would be attending.

"So little brother, I'm looking over this list of invites and I don't see Angelique's name on here. What's up with that?"

As he ironed his dress shirt for the funeral, just hearing her name made him burn his finger. Although he heard what she said, he acted as if he didn't and continued with his ironing. Tanya walked over and snatched the dress shirt from under the iron.

"What the hell?"

"What do you mean what the hell? I asked you a question. Why isn't Angelique coming?"

He walked over to his couch and hugged his cushion, knowing his sister would be upset. "The next issue of the magazines main focus is in Europe and she has a big meeting, some negotiation meeting tonight and she couldn't make the trip." "Wow! She's trifling. No offence bro."

Nathan looked up at his sister as she folded the last of the programs and put the lid on the box. "Don't look at me like that. Your fiancés parents both died, they were just murdered or whatever you want to call it!' She Yelled. 'And you can't bring your ass on a plane to come and pay your respects OR be there for your fiancé? Come on Nate, if that's somebody you want to be married to do you. But to me that's bullshit."

He stood up and put on his shirt and as he started to button up his top he spoke, "So what do you want me to do, call off the engagement? They didn't even like her."

"SO, it has nothing to do with her, it's about you. Your feelings and how this is affecting you."

He threw on his sweater vest and looked at her. "You're right, it has nothing to do with her, it's about me. And I'm going to be there, that's all that matters."

Tanya looked at her brother who was in total denial of where his relationship or marriage stood. She was thirty and a woman at that, so she knew the ins and outs of a relationship. Maybe it had something to do with the fact that she was his sister why he didn't feel comfortable with expressing himself with her. But that was just how Nathan was. He couldn't open up with you, especially if he knew you were right.

Nathan knew she was right and he hated having to deal with his family or what was left of it, reminding him how wrong it was that she didn't come there. He knew that much already.

After Tanya got dressed, she received a phone call from their Aunt Erin. Nathan walked back in from loading the last of the boxes in his car.

"Aunty Erin just called."

"Oh yeah. What she say?"

She picked up her purse and brought her sunglasses down to the brim of her nose, "Her flight just got in from England, and she'll be at the church in half an hour." Tanya looked at him and smiled, "What do you know, England's in which continent? Europe."

His sister walked outside and he rolled his eyes at her attempt to make him feel bad. Good attempt, because he did.

They drove to the church in silence. Tanya turned on the radio and listened to Mariah Carey and Boys ll Men's collaboration, One Sweet Day. From the corner of his eyes, Nathan could see his sister break down publicly, for the first time since he told her. She wasn't bawling she contained her emotions very well, considering she had a better relationship with her parents.

She was a very successful business woman for the top law firm in Atlanta. She interacted with celebrities and people who acted like, well, their shit don't stink. But the best part about it all, was that Tanya never acted like that. Although she was in the midst of that 6 days a week, possibly 14 hours a day, she remained the little girl her mom and dad molded her into.

She moved out and left Nathan when she was 21 and he was 18. Tanya always visited her parents, and even visited her brother and she was caught in the middle of them all. The neutral party. It was no wonder that it bothered her so much that her soon to be sister-in-law dissed not only her parents and herself, but her baby brother. If Nathan thought his sister was going to let it slide with just one smart remark, he was in way over his head.

They got to the church and it was like a flower heaven. There were several flower arrangements and the two caskets were set up side by side both with flower arrangements in front and a bouquet on each end. Tanya just looked around and looked at her brother to explain. The Pastor approached them and hugged them both.

"Pastor Rose, it looks beautiful in here. Who did this?"

He smiled, "A lovely young lady your brother knows. Ask him, she came in here early this morning, set it all up on her own and headed out for a nine o'clock meeting."

Tanya smiled, thinking it was Angelique.

"Well Nate, Angelique came through after all."

"No, it wasn't Angelique. It was Casey."

"Moms Casey?"

Nathan looked at her, "You know her?"

"Well yeah, mom introduced me to her way back when. How do you think I landed my job in Atlanta?"

Pastor Rose looked at them both and excused himself from their conversation. Tanya walked up to look at her parents and Nathan placed the boxes on a nearby table, and then joined his sister at the front.

"I can't believe their gone Nate."

"Me neither." He held his sister by her shoulder as she broke down, this time more tears fell from her eyes.

After an hour of setting up, people began to arrive. Aunts, uncles, close friends, friends from work, and even Tanya's husband flew in from Atlanta that morning with their daughter, Eve. She was named after their late mother, Evelyn.

Nathan saw his boys walk into the church shortly after his niece and brother in law arrived. He had a few moments before the ceremony started, so he decided to mingle a little.

"Hey Fellas." The boys all hugged him and Steven replied.

"What's going on Nate, you look good."

"Yeah Nate, it looks amazing in here. You hire a decorator?" Shawn asked.

Nathan replied, "Nah, this girl, my mom knows did it."

They nodded in understanding and for a second they didn't know what to say.

Then Gregory spoke, "Where's the wifey? I want to say my hellos."

The boys all agreed, and looked around the church.

"Nate, I don't see her."

Nathan turned and looked around, "Neither do I. Excuse me boys." Nathan said and walked to the front of the church where his sister was chatting to her aunts and uncles. Nathan walked over and hugged a few of his relatives and engaged in brief conversation with a very fake smile on his face.

His friends still looked over at him and Steven spoke, "Is she seriously not here?"

They walked over and sat in one of the pews and started their own conversation. "Well, put it this way.' Gregory answered, 'If Miss. Angel was here, she'd be all over his ass right now."

Shawn shook his head and commented, "I aint saying she's a gold digger."

Steven was probably the closest to Nathan. He knew all of the Nathan and Angelique troubles, in the past. And it hurt him to see that she wasn't there, so he could imagine what Nathan felt. He knew how much Nathan put on the line for her and how much love he had for her. And as his best friend, he knew how pissed off Nathan had to of been. "That girl is fucking around."

Shawn and Gregory looked at Steven in shock.

"Bro, you're in the house of Jesus." Shawn reminded him.

"Yeah, that's where Angelique needs to find her ass too. If she wants any form of mercy on her soul."

The boys sat back and realized that Steven was upset for Nathan and they were as well. Angelique was dissing Nathan to his face, to their face and to his entire family. And she didn't even realize it.

The ceremony began with a bible reading from little 7 year old Eve who adored her grandparents as much as they adored her.

She read; *The LORD is my shepherd; I shall not want. He maketh me to lie down in green pastures: he leadeth me beside the still waters. He restoreth my soul: he leadeth me in the paths of righteousness for his name's sake. Yea, though I walk through the valley of the shadow of death, I will fear no evil: for thou art with me; thy rod and thy staff they comfort me. Thou preparest a table before me in the presence of mine enemies: thou anointest my head with oil; my cup runneth over. Surely goodness and mercy shall follow me all the days of my life: and I will dwell in the house of the LORD for ever.*

As she finished, Pastor Rose approached the podium and welcomed everyone to the celebration of the lives of Jeffery & Evelyn Walker. The choir sung Amazing Grace.

They chose Amazing Grace because that was the song Evelyn sung lead to, her very first time joining the choir. And their father, Jeffery played it on the piano for her, their first date. It was like their good luck song.

As the choir sung and the pianist played, Tanya broke down and held tight to her husband and her brother as little Eve held onto her daddy.

Nathan cried, but cried on the inside, he needed to deliver his eulogy momentarily and couldn't go up there soft and wounded. He needed to be strong for his family and be as strong as his parents knew he could be.

As he approached the podium he looked out into the crowd and saw everyone but his Angel. Even his life long friends showed up and made time out of their busy schedules. And he shook his head and began.

"Good afternoon everyone. My name is" he looked up and saw Casey walk in. She wore a bright green wool jacket. She took it off and wore a black corset with a blazer, black skinny legged dress pants with black and gold stilettos. He stuttered and then realized he was in the middle of his speech.

"Um, Nathan Walker, son of Evelyn and Jeffery Walker. My sister Tanya and I would like to thank you all for coming. It means so much to us…to know that you all loved and cared for my parents." The crowd cheered a little and he continued, "I would personally like to thank Casey Green for making time out of her busy schedule to attend today and decorate the church as beautifully as she did. I appreciate it and I'm sure everyone else agrees with me when I say it's an amazing sight to look at." The congregation agreed with him with their cheers and she blew him a kiss and he smiled at her.

"I never thought I would be here, so soon. I'm only 27 and I feel like I didn't get enough time to spend with them. A part of me blames myself. No. A big part of me blames myself and I cant imagine what the next 27 years are going to be without my dad telling me that the Raptors lost again or my mom calling me her Baby in front of all of you I'm sure, even though I'm old enough to have my own baby."

The crowd laughed and smiled, which gave Nathan the courage to continue. He let out a huge sigh and kept going. "I don't know if they knew how much they meant to me but, they made me into who I am, and I'm proud of who I am. I'm proud of who my sister is and we owe that to these two individuals, who" He broke down. "Who were taken from us within like 15 minutes? And it breaks my heart to see my sister and my niece and all of you here crying because I could use their guidance and support right about now. I'm not a man who asks for assistance very often if at all. And I realize now how hard it is without my mom and dad here, beside me, behind me but most importantly alive, well and with me. With all of us. You all feel as though you lost a piece of your life. I feel like I lost my whole life, because if it wasn't for them, where would I be? No where. And now that they aren't here does that mean I no longer have a reason to go on, because my greatness sprung from them?"

He stopped and turned to his parents' casket. He looked at how peaceful his mom and dad both looked. Then he thought back to the night they were both murdered and he started to cry. Slow tears, tears of pain, anger and regret. "I witnessed the death of my mom and my dad." Some members of the church gasped and others just stared at him with tears. "It felt like my world had just ended and killing myself was the only option left. It all happened so fast and I couldn't move, my legs couldn't move. I couldn't save her, I couldn't save him. I can't even remember if I tried. It all happened so fast and I apologize to all of you for not being a stronger man to move my legs and…" Tears just flooded his eyes and he lost it. "Stop everything. I love them, no matter what anyone thinks or what they thought I loved them. And as I sat in their blood and cursed the day I was born, I laughed so I wouldn't cry. I laughed so I could wake up from this dream. I laughed so it wouldn't hurt so bad and I laugh now because they were right and I realize today" and he looked at Casey "they were right." Trying hard to hold it together he said, "I'm sorry, I can't do this."

He walked off stage and left the ceremony for some air outside. The remainder of the congregation just let him go. Witnessing the murder of both parents was exceptionally hard and everyone understood what he was probably going through.

Casey followed him and let him breathe for a minute and then walked over to him and hugged him. "I need you to stop blaming yourself." She reached into her purse and pulled out a letter.

"What's this?"

"A letter your mom had the intention to send to you, a couple years back."

"Why didn't she send it and why do you have it?"

Casey sighed and turned her back to him, "She gave it to me and said to keep it, for she will send it when she thinks you're ready to hear the truth. She didn't want you to run home and throw all your dreams away and get worried."

Nathan believed her. His mother always kept things away from him and Tanya while they were away at school with the crazy thought they would run home.

After reading the letter, he realized that he probably would have.

Dear Nathan,

How's school going sweetie? I just want you to know that your father and I are very proud of you and all that you are now and what you will become. I was wishing I could tell you this in person but it's hard to say without crying. Your father is battling his illness of Schizophrenia. And its bad baby, sometimes he doesn't think straight or he doesn't even know what he's saying. I don't want to alarm you or your sister, I think we can handle it and get through it in time before it worsens. I need you to be strong though. I'm as strong as I can be. I love you to death Nathan. And I want you to know, none of this has anything to do with you or your sister.

Love you ALWAYS

Mom x o x o

The letter was dated 3 months before he graduated Law School and started his career. The peak in his life. The beginning of his life. He looked at Casey as she began to tear up. "If she sent this letter, I would have left."

She nodded, "She knew you would."

He took the letter and put it in his pocket and walked back into the church with Casey. He headed back to the front and hugged his niece as she cried as they brought the caskets out the door. His sister whispered, "It's not your fault baby brother."

He held her hand, "I know."

He looked at his dad being carried out in the casket and looked at him, "I'm sorry I wasn't there for you dad."

They had the dinner reception at Nathans house. The dinner table was filled with food. More food than anyone had in mind. There was salmon, steak, ribs, barbeque chicken, rice and peas, corn, potato salad, chicken parmesan with noodles and seven different juices and liquor. Someone must of figured, drinking away there miseries in the alcohol would heal the grief of their loss.

Nathan sat with the guys for a while, when he noticed Casey and Tanya talking. Casey was holding a champagne glass and as he approached them, she excused her self to make a public announcement.

"Excuse me everyone." Everyone stopped and faced her. "Hi, my name is Casey Green." Steven, Shawn and Gregory cheered her on, remembering what Nathan said about her at the ceremony. Soon, everyone joined in remembering the same event. She blushed, "Thank you. I would like everyone to raise you're glasses of champagne, juice, rum and coke, whatever it may be, to the skies above to our loved ones, Jeffery and Evelyn Walker. We are to celebrate their lives, not mourn." She looked over at Nathan. "For every mans loss is another's gain. And today ladies and gentlemen, our loss is his gain." She said looking towards the heaven above her. "Take care of them for us. Thank you."

Everyone smiled and shouted "Cheers." Tanya looked at her brother who was in awe, over the speech.

Casey walked over to them and she hugged Tanya and looked at Nathan. "I'm sorry to leave like this, but I have to run. I have an important appointment I can't miss. Take care." Nathan nodded and smiled at her. He wasn't sure what he should say to her. "Thank you, for coming and for, the flowers and for the speech and the letter."

He looked over at his sister, who just beamed. "Honestly, thank you. I'm glad you could make it."

Casey buttoned up her wool coat and shook her head, "Honestly, it was my pleasure."

Tanya interrupted, "Case, it's 7:30, you have an appointment this late?"

"Girl, we all know the needy never rest."

They laughed and Nathan just admired her. As she noticed, he quickly sipped his champagne and turned his head towards his friends who were watching him the entire time. They laughed at him and he was embarrassed.

Casey left very politely and Tanya ran back over to her brother who sat back down with his boys and Devon. "Can I talk to you Nate?" He looked around like, why not? "What letter did Casey give to you, or whatever?" The boys all hyped up and he brushed them off.

"Not that kind of note perverts. And did you guys forget I was engaged?"

Gregory spoke sarcastically, "We didn't, but it's obvious a certain female did." Ouch. Nathan thought, he knew he was referring to Angelique, but Gregory didn't care, he was one who never took no shit from no girl. And Angelique's behavior, agreed, was very shitty.

Tanya just assumed that Casey and Nathan had a thing for each other, but she didn't know the true contents of the letter. So she made assumptions. "So if it's not like that, let me see the letter." Tanya insisted.

Devon entered the conversation, "Honey, what happens between those two, is strictly, between those two sweetie. Do you show them our love letters?"

She rolled her eyes. "Come on Nate."

"Where we going? It was a letter from mom, explaining that dad was a Schizophrenic! He was fucking crazy and she didn't tell us because she knew we'd hop out of school and hop on the next train to come to the rescue. And throw all our shit away. She hid it from us because she figured they could just deal with it before it got, well got to this point, where we're sitting at their funeral. He didn't murder mom, some fucker in his head did!"

Nathan got up and walked over to the dessert table. Tanya stood there and tears filled her eyes as she looked at the boys and her husband looking back at her with the same regret in their eyes.

She wiped her tears and walked over to her brother as he put some fresh fruits on his plate. "Sorry." He put the plate down and hugged his sister.

"Me too."

CHAPTER FIVE

I Could Beat Myself

The week of spring break, the remainder of the Walker family took a trip to Florida. Tanya thought it would be good way to get the death of her grandparents off her daughters mind.

After a week of having fun, laughing, reminiscing and the occasional sleeping, spring break came to an end.

As Eve slept and Tanya's husband Devon went out for some take out, his wife and brother in law packed the suit cases. "Although you cried like a baby Nate, you were amazing."

He laughed and threw a wet bathing suit at his sister. "Yeah well, I hear the ladies like that sensitive shit, and I thought I might as well give it a try."

She smiled, "It was sweet what Casey did."

"I know the flowers were incredible."

That definitely was not what his sister had in mind. "I was referring to her canceling her conference and coming to the church early to set up and then head out for a nine o'clock client meeting."

He looked at his sister. "Not this again Tanya, please. She didn't do it for me, she did it for mom."

"Didn't she though? You went to see her. You asked her for help. You asked her to be there. You rushed out of the church and she came to comfort you. Hell, sounds like she came there for you."

He took note of her foolish points and shook it off. "She came there to pay her respects to mom. She did all those things because she cared for mom and she's a nice person. For crying out loud she's a Social Worker. Her job is to make sure people are okay and are open with themselves."

His sister zipped up her suitcase and spoke, "That's where you're wrong. She is a Social Worker and one of the owners of that corporation that she runs. Now how is it that she could get out of a conference that she organized for months but your little fiancé couldn't miss one meeting for a magazine, that isn't even published until next month? Think about it." And he did. It drove him crazy that night as he slept or tried to. And at the same time, all he could do was sit there and try and defend her in his mind. He tried to make excuses and justify reasons as to why she would do this to him. As much as his blood boiled to admit this, his sister was right. And he couldn't sleep well until he found out from Angelique why that was so.

He sat on the stool of the villa that they stayed in and spun around. His niece walked over to him. "You okay Uncle Nate? You look terrrrrrrible."

He laughed, "Yes E-V-E Ima be alright."

"You still miss grandma and grandpa?"

"Oh Yeah, more than you can imagine." He didn't sound too convincing to his niece and she picked that up.

"Is it about Angelique, your girlllllfriend?"

He pulled on her pigtail and chased her into the living room. "NO girls have cooties. Grosse."

'Am I cootiefull Uncle Nate?'

Nathan laughed at the word 'cootiefull'. 'I don't even know how you came up with that word boo, but yes, you're the cootiefull queen.' He watched as his niece laughed with such enthusiasm. He remembered when he was her age, everything was just so, simple. He'd give anything to get that back, right now.

They arrived at the airport and Nate pulled his sister and brother in law aside as his niece bent down to tie her laces. "Guys I hate to bail, I know you're going to miss me on the flight home. But I'm going to take a different flight."

Devon held onto his wife and said, "Hey that's cool my brotha, I would like to sit next to my two favorite ladies in the world anyhow."

The guys both laughed and Tanya looked up to her brother and looked concerned. "I'm going to stop in Paris. I have some things I need to settle." She nodded and then hugged her brother.

"You be careful and call us when you get in."

"Girl I'm a grown man bout be careful. I'll be alright. Gonna go get my wife back." Nathan joked with his sister and headed on his way. Tanya's smile was a little unsure.

He arrived in Paris the next morning around 7:00am, too tired to even think about this confrontation. As soon as he got through at the airport he took a cab to the nearest tourist hotel. He booked a room and slept for about an hour, until his cell phone vibrated, it was Angelique.

"Hi baby did I wake you?"

"Actually yes, yes you did." She laughed at what she thought was humor.

"I'm sorry."

He sat up. "For what?"

She sounded a little confused, "For waking you up."

He looked over at his clock and realized it was 9:30am and he was ready to just go home and be around shit he was use to. "Where are you staying Angelique?"

"The Country Side Hotel."

He laughed out loud, "Good that's where I'm at, meet me in my hotel room 556 in twenty minutes. Don't be late. Love you."

And he hung up. He jumped into the shower and put on his Sean John cologne, with his light blue Parasuco jeans, and a black t-shirt. His intentions were to have a nice chat with his fiancé, they would make up and all would be grand again. And he could be on his way and go home.

The door knocked and at that moment, everything flooded his mind. What should he say, how should he say it, should he say it? He didn't know if he was doing this for himself, his mother, his father, his sister or for her, but he knew he had to do it or it would forever be on his mind.

He opened the door to see his beautiful fiancé dressed in a bright blue summer dress and a white head band in her wavy hair. He kissed his chocolate beauty, held her hand and led her to his room. "You smell nice." She said as they held each other and just stared into each others eyes.

"You look nice."

She giggled and modeled around his room while he took it all in. How her hair was just flowing, her legs freshly moisturized with some type of oil and her breast just looked perky and full of life.

He sat on his bed and took off his shirt, knowing how to play with his fiancés mind. Instantly, she climbed on top of him, with her c cupped breast in his face. He gave each of them a kiss and she smiled as her eyes rolled back in her head as he removed them from the dress and sucked each nipple.

He zipped down her dress as she attacked his neck with her tongue and rubbed her hands along his thighs. She whispered how much she missed him and he whispered the same. As his lips met hers and they were intertwined in a passionate lip lock that no man or woman could stop at that moment. She pulled away and sucked on his ear. "How was your meeting baby?"

As he threw her to the bed to ease his way into her that early morning, he made his way to her neck and began to slurp rather harshly. And she whispered, "It was moved to the next day, baby."

Within those eight words his dick became limp and he got off of her. She looked at him with her dress covering half her body. "Baby why'd you stop?"

"Better question why the hell didn't you come?"

She laughed, "You didn't give me the chance to."

"TO THE FUNERAL DAMMIT ANGELIQUE!"

He threw his shirt back on, stood over her as she sat up and zipped back up her dress. "I don't know. I guess I didn't think of it."

"You didn't think of me?"

"Well yeah I thought of you Nathan. You're all I think about."

He turned away from her. He couldn't believe what he was hearing. "The last conversation we had was about my parents DYING and you not being able to miss some fucking meeting to be there. And when the meeting was cancelled, you flying out DIDN'T ENTER YOUR MIND?"

"I had other things to take care of."

"How could you have other things to take care of if the meeting was suppose to happen that day? I can't believe you right now I cant believe the amount of shit you're bringing to me and my life right now."

"It's the truth Nate."

"THE TRUTH! You want to know the truth. I saw my father murder my mother and then fucking murder himself, and that, that's YOUR FAULT!"

He picked up his bags and moved to the door. She ran over and locked it as he opened it. "Stop it Nathan!"

"Get out of my face. I can't even look at you. I don't even know who you are."

"It's me baby, it's Angel." She pleaded.

"Angel? I needed a fucking Angel that night and you weren't there. You didn't even call me! I'm busy too. But I still call you. I still miss you. I still wish you were there every fucking second of it. Everyone else had someone to hold and cry on. I held onto my fucking jock for crying out loud."

She started to cry, "Don't yell at me. What do you want from me? I'm not perfect, it was a mistake."

"It was the worst mistake you could have made. Just like my mistake was proposing to a selfish girl like YOU!"

It felt like the electricity blew and silence was among them. She looked away out of embarrassment and said, "You don't want to marry me?" Nathan just sat there in silence; he couldn't believe what he said. And he didn't know if he regretted it either. "Well, with that answer I don't think we should get married."

She placed the ring in his hand and said, "We need some time apart."

"When I need you the most right now, you're going to give me that lame ass excuse."

"What do you want me to say?"

"I don't know, for starters SORRY might work. But you're not even sorry. I am." He got up and walked to the front door. "When I leave, count on me, COUNT ON ME not coming back! It's done after this."

She watched as her ex fiancé walked out the door. She didn't even flinch. She didn't even cry. Hell, she didn't even care. She wiped the last tear from her face and watched him get into a cab from the window. And just like that he was gone.

CHAPTER SIX

Nine to Five

Monday March 19th came faster than Nathan had anticipated. He couldn't find it in himself to gather what was worse, the fact that his parents are gone and his fiancé didn't show, or the fact the she didn't care enough to show.

It didn't matter now anyways, he had to focus on getting back into the swing of things down at the firm and boy did he have a lot to get caught up on.

"Good Morning Mr. Walker. Here is your coffee. The big boss is on line one; you have a meeting at three thirty. The trial you have scheduled on your birthday, I courteously moved it to the weekend after and all the paper work on your desk needs to be approved by yourself with a signature and your client prior to your loss has found another representative AND welcome back!"

"A new representative? Why, what was wrong with how we were handling it?"

"The mother of the little criminal got worried and anxious to get the case under control I guess." Victoria smiled and hoped Nathan followed through on her humor.

He laughed, "Thanks Victoria. It's good to be back."

He opened his office door placed his brief case on his side table and put his mug down beside it. He then took the call on line one and moved his papers over to the side table and got to work.

He called Victoria into his office after about an hour of paper work. "What's up Nate? Can I call you Nate, is that okay?"

He looked at her and smiled, "Victoria that's okay, calm down, I won't eat you."

"Good because I don't taste that great. Not that, anyone has ever told me that I taste bad but, I'm a person and I just figured I wouldn't be as good as chicken, or juice."

She stopped and Nathan just looked at her like, what the hell. "Sorry." He could tell she was really embarrassed and he was embarrassed for her as well.

"How were things while I was gone?"

"I saved all your voice messages."

"How many did I receive?"

"About thirty eight."

He looked up, "Wow! That many?"

"Yup I saved them all for you, and the few that would be erased by the time you got back today, I wrote them down electronically for you out front and I emailed you a copy of the message, the number, the name of the contact and the date and time it was left. Anything else sir?"

He smiled. She was a very pretty and very intelligent individual and still, so dumb, for a lack of a better word. "Yes, could you just call me as a reminder as to when I should head up for the meeting today, just in case I fall behind and lose track of time?"

She nodded and walked off.

He looked over some documents for his upcoming trial and couldn't focus right. The past three weeks felt like such a blur to him. He started to question if it even happened. But it did and this was now his reality. He had lost three people within that time along with his outlook on life and relationships. He just couldn't believe that this was the way life was going to be. He still couldn't get past how fast it all changed.

He started to relate himself to a criminal. He saw how easily he could be free and then like that, behind bars, facing criminal charges with life taken away from you. He was just like a criminal, minus the criminal acts of course, he was as lifeless as a criminal. Except unlike them, he had no one to represent him for his fiancé chose a path that excluded him, completely.

He walked out of his office and headed down the street for a hot chocolate in the nearest Tim Horton's. "Hi, could I get a large hot chocolate and an everything bagel with cream cheese and tomatoes."

"Sure that's 2.91 please."

The woman behind him said, "Make that two large hot chocolates with two everything bagels with cream cheese and tomatoes."

He turned around and it was Casey. "I got it."

She paid for the drinks and bagels and they found a seat. "If I didn't know better, I'd say that you're either stalking me or reading my mind."

"Or the other way around." He joked back with her.

"So how's your first day back to work? This is your first day back right?"

He nodded, "How'd you know?"

"Well when my mother past away last may, my first day back, I sat in this exact seat, and enjoyed a large hot chocolate and an everything bagel, except it had extra cream cheese. Okay and a vanilla sprinkle donut. And instead of you sitting in front of me, I called my older brother so he could mope with me." She smiled and sipped her beverage.

"I'm sorry to hear that, I know how hard it must have been."

"Not as hard as people make you believe it should be. But your strong and your just in a bad situation Nathan, you'll make it through the mess, the pain, everything."

Again, she spoke with such confidence and professionalism in her voice. He almost felt like he was reading a book and everything just flowed so well and things that wouldn't make sense to him if he read alone did, for it was being read aloud. "Well I trust you on that."

"And what you don't trust anything else I say?"

Laughing he confessed, "Nope, pretty girls I meet only want one thing from me."

"And what's that?"

He answered as if it was obvious, "Well, me."

She stretched her hands over the table she said "Call the cops; have me arrested because I think I'm guilty of that offence. Oh but you have to be my lawyer too because your mom told me you're all that and a bag of chips." Casey snapped her fingers in exaggeration.

She was instantly attracted to Nathan from the first day she met him and she's not an idiot, she could feel him undressing her with his eyes then and she could feel him doing it now. She was single, and a successful man was definitely her type.

Laughing again at her humor, he kissed her left hand and then her right and she pulled them back into her lap. She watched him as he bit into his bagel and he had cream cheese at the corner of his mouth. "Well, to answer your initial question, I lost a client today and I'm pretty bummed out about it."

"Big money eh?"

He smirked, 'Oh yeah. And there's nothing worse then losing a client that's bringing in the BIG MONEY!"

She licked her thumb and reached over the table and wiped the corner of his mouth. In the midst of it she realized what she was doing. She leaned back and had nothing but regret on her face. "Oh my God, I'm sorry, I'm just so use to taking care of my niece and nephew that, oh my God I'm such a mom. I'm sorry Nathan."

He took her hand and before she wiped it off in her napkin, he brought her thumb to his lips and sucked off the cream cheese. "It's okay."

Butterflies took over her body and she grabbed her hot chocolate with hopes that it would eliminate the excitement in the pits of her stomach. Nothing. They were still there, if not more. Because the way he looked at her, she felt naked. She felt as though she was naked and her mhmmm's were showing and he liked it.

Smiling, he asked her, "What are you doing tonight?"

"Um, uhhh, nothing. My last client appointment ends at five."

"Cool, let's go do something. I want to thank you for buying me… brunch; I guess that's what you could call this."

She nodded hesitantly still shocked at what he asked her.

"You okay Casey?"

"Yeah, I'm good."

He looked at his watch and said "Okay, should I pick you up or do you want to meet there?"

"We could meet up. I have to swing by my brothers for a minute, so it would probably be easier if I drove."

He wrote down the address on a napkin and slid it to her like it was a secret note and they were in the tenth grade. She giggled and he commented on her smile, "Now don't think I'm trying to be corny, but your smile, it redefines stunning."

She got up and put her coat on, "Well me and my stunning smile will see you later, Mr. Walker. And it was corny." She winked at him and walked out.

He sat there in awe at how one spirited woman could just change his mind, change his views, and change him. Let's not push the situation, but she had some sort of hold on his heart. For he only felt like himself when she was around. He didn't think about his loss or his faults when she was there because Casey made him feel as if none of that shit mattered. The three times they interacted, every single time, she made him feel like his life wasn't half bad. And really, it wasn't.

He headed back to work with a spring in his step and a lift in his spirit. He got to work and was wrapped up in a telephone conversation that lasted about an hour and a half.

Knock, Knock! "Sorry to bother you Nate, but your three thirty meeting, will begin in about 60 seconds." She made eye contact and nodded as Nathan nodded to let her know he will be right along. "Okay I understand the changes you want to be made and they will be made as soon as I get out of this meeting Mrs. Coleman."

He scribbled some words on a piece of paper and then kindly got off the phone with his client. He quickly flew up several flights of stairs to make it to his meeting with the rest of the gentlemen at his firm. The meeting lasted about half an hour. They welcomed him back and sent there deepest regrets and blessings to him and his sister on such an incredible loss.

To take care of business they just handled some paper work pertaining to their trial dates, the bookings of the courts and random discussions about which judge they did and did not want to get.

"How's your fiancé handling your loss?" His boss asked him, as he was about to make his way through the door.

"Better than I am sir."

Nathans smile was as fake as the toupee his boss wore to cover up the fact that the company was stressing him out and he was losing not only his mind, but his hair.

He headed out of the office that evening at about five o'clock. He flew home, took a shower, and threw on his khakis with a white and gold LRG top and white and gold air forces with a white hooded sweater. He looked in the mirror and realized that Angelique had bought him that shirt, the first time they exchanged gifts. He quickly threw it off and jumped into his walk in closet for another outfit.

As he anxiously searched for the perfect outfit, he remembered his first date with Angelique. They went bowling and he remembered her wearing all white. It was a shame she didn't know the alley had those black glow in the dark lights that loved the colour white. Nathan laughed at her all night and she was so embarrassed.

He smiled to himself, in the memory. But that was it. It was just a memory.

He decided to go to the drive in movies with Casey, for a change of scenery and for his own selfish reason that he'd never been to a drive in before. He gave Casey instructions to drive across the street from the drive in at the McDonalds, park there and he would meet her there. He pulled up beside her dark green 2008 Maserati Quattro Porte Sports Car.

Nathans mouthed dropped into his lap. Getting out of his car he spoke, "Holy shit, this is how we living?"

She laughed, "Yes it is. This is my baby. But, look who's talking Mr. I drive a 2008 Mercedes Benz."

He laughed and hopped back in his car. "SL 65, thank you very much." They both realized it wasn't a bad thing that he was as proud of his car as she was with hers.

She laughed with him. "Let me guess, you're favorite colour is green?" She buckled up and he looked at her with her hair in a tight bun with side swept bang, huge gold hoop earrings, and a black jean jumpsuit with green flats and her green and gold Coach purse.

"Yes green is my favorite colour. Is it obvious?"

He inhaled her scent and it was definitely one of Victoria's secrets that he couldn't help but want to get to know it. "Naw, it's not obvious at all. Are you sure your last name is Green, or you just say it is because your real last name is something awkward like, Pussywillow?"

She played around with her gold necklace and laughed at his dumb statement. Shaking her head she answered, "I'm positive my last name is Green and me liking the colour is merely a coincidence."

They drove into the lot and discovered it was a surprise screening of a new horror movie *Beyond the grave of Millicent Monroe*. "I hate horror movies."

"Aw they scare you?"

"No!" she spat at him, "I just think they're stupid and they are sooooo fake and yes, they scare me, sometimes."

She expected him to laugh but he didn't. "I respect that I guess, we can leave, if you want."

"No, that's okay. We can stay." She admired his sensitivity.

He sensed that she was extremely uncomfortable and wanted nothing more but to get the hell out of there. "Tell you what. We won't turn on the radio. We'll watch the screen play and we'll make our own noises and narration to the film, for the next hour and 45 minutes. What do you say?"

She looked at the screen and turned towards Nathan, "Cool, as long as I get to be the pretty one."

"Well, that's a mistake sweetie, because everyone knows the pretty ones always die first or get killed the worse!"

"Not this time, and even if that's what happens on the screen. I'll still be here in your car. Safe. With you."

Anyone else would have felt completely awkward in the car at this time but they were compelled to stare at one another by no one else but themselves. Eye contact is weird, which would only mean TOO much eye contact is just down right scary.

Nathan soon regained consciousness and reached into the back seat of his BMW and retrieved a blanket. "Look at that, it's green."

She gasped, "You just made my night, Mr. Walker."

About half way through the movie and their ridiculous narrations that completely contradicted with the story line, they decided to move to the back seat of the car. Once they got there Casey joked, "No guy has ever invited me to the back seat of his car before."

"I know, I'm a gentleman, what can I say?"

They finally decided to actually watch the movie because it looked as though it was more interesting than they gave it credit for. By the end of the night he had his arm around Casey and her head was resting peacefully on his chest. Amused by the movie, they didn't even notice the passion they had created between them with just a blanket and their two bodies. It just felt natural to be sitting in that position for the hour for they realized their arrangement only, when the movie had ended.

Casey slowly got up and fixed up her hair and sat in silence beside him. They acted like a bunch of teenagers who just had sex for the first time and were experiencing the awkwardness.

He bent over to fix his shoe lace and all Casey could think about was the rock hard chest she was just laying on and why her hands froze when it could have been warmed up by the fire his chest confined. Nathan hopped out and went to the driver seat, and she soon followed and sat in the front passenger seat. "Good movie." She broke the silence.

"Yeah, didn't think it would have been that good." He confessed.

He reached her Maserati across the street and she sighed, "Well this is me. Thanks for tonight, the movie, the ride, the popcorn, the laughter. It felt good to laugh."

He agreed, "Yeah it was good to laugh, but the pleasure was all mine, Miss. Green."

And it really was, for he saw things in her that he never took the time to see in any woman; her humor, her intelligence but most importantly her enthusiasm for life and regaining control of it by living it.

Of course she didn't say that, but those were the vibes he took from her and he never got vibes from any one other than Angelique. But those vibes never appeared that quickly.

She said goodnight and blew Nathan a kiss as she hopped into her car. He waited for her to drive off and as she did, he reversed and drove home.

CHAPTER SEVEN

Wednesday Afternoons

It has now been a month since his parents died and Nathan was impressed at how far along he had made it without them. He only had two breakdowns since the morning things ended with Angelique and every time, Casey was there to comfort him.

When Nathan got his 12 o'clock lunch break he decided to take a drive down to the cemetery where his parents were buried just weeks earlier. As he walked what seemed like a treacherous walk from the parking lot to the area his parents were located in, he thought of what he wanted to say. He ran a few things off in his mind that he would tell his mom and what he would tell his father. Still all the words in his head, just made no sense. He approached his moms' grave and noticed Casey standing there in silence and then she spoke.

"Hi, Mrs. Walker. It's me Casey." She sighed. "I miss you like crazy, but I met your son and every time we interact I see a piece of you that lives in him and I feel safe and protected, because I see he wouldn't hurt me and I know you always had the best interests at heart for me. But I wanted to tell you that, the company is going well, thanks to the countless amount of work you had done, you made it easy for me to function on my own until my new secretary arrived. Don't worry, she's nothing compared to you."

She laughed, "Truth is, she's kinda sloppy and weird." She tried to hold back her tears and as she moved her hair out of her face she fell apart. "I needed you to be there for me Evelyn. What am I suppose to do now?" She looked at her surroundings and noticed Nathan looking down at his mothers' grave.

She quickly wiped her tears and he walked over to her, "Don't. Don't worry about it, I'm here." He held her as she cried on his shoulder and through her tears she managed to say, "I loved her more than I loved myself most days. When my mom died, she was there for me when I didn't want to be at work. I didn't want to go on and she brought me through it. Whose gonna bring me through this?" He wiped her tears and she looked at him.

"Come, let's go sit down. "

He held her hand and walked with her over to the nearest park bench. She sat down and he sat right beside her. "I'm sorry; I didn't mean to fall apart in front of you like that. I just couldn't handle it anymore; you don't know how close your mom and I were."

He held her hand, "Don't apologize."

For some reason she felt awkward with the situation they were in, but at the same time she liked it. "We use to talk about you and Tanya, almost everyday. I knew you before I even met you Nate." Nathan, looked at her for her to continue, he wanted to know if she knew about Angelique. "I saw graduation pictures and birthday pictures and I felt like I knew you. Maybe that's why; I can be myself around you. Maybe that's why; we connected so easily when we met." Nathan didn't know what to say. He couldn't explain how he was feeling at that point and time, but Nathan knew it was a feeling to strong to just ignore. Casey continued, "After I met Tanya in 2002, I knew I wanted to meet you. If you were anything like your mother, I knew you had to be, full of passion, full of life and, here you are."

She lifted her head up at him as she spoke and slowly he pressed his lips against hers and they kissed. Five Mississippi's later, they pulled apart and Nathan responded by saying, "I'm glad I'm here with you." She leaned in again and kissed him, this time with more lust, excitement and...slobber.

When they realized they were in a cemetery they stopped and with their foreheads still pressing together they laughed and she kissed him gently one last time. "I should go."

He stood up out of awkwardness, "I'm actually surprised to see you here, I didn't see your car." She stood up and pushed her hands into the pocket of her coat and swayed back and fourth for a minute.

"Yeah, I decided to take a walk, a long walk. And it just felt right to come you know? Every Wednesday Evelyn and I would take a walk and go out for lunch and I don't know." She shrugged, "I feel like I owe it to her to visit her, Wednesdays were our days."

Her tears were all dried up now and she stood tall and confident. Opening up, made her feel stronger and at ease, probably the same way her clients felt after a session with her.

Nathan kept his focus to the ground where his parent both laid and he held it together and didn't cry. It's not that he didn't want to or feel to, he now had found the strength to do without crying. "Crying won't bring them back." He told Casey as well as himself. She nodded after a single tear fell from her eye and rolled down her cheek.

"She wouldn't want us to be crying, she'd want us to be rejoicing because we still have life here to be lived." That warmed Nathans heart because other than his sister Tanya, Casey knew as much as he knew about his mother if not more. And it was comforting to have her around, for it's almost as if his mother never left.

She walked over to him and put both her hands, into one of each of his coat pockets. She reached up to kiss him on his cheek and she whispered, "Thank You."

She walked away from him and as she neared the exit of the cemetery she turned, kissed her hand and waved goodbye to Nathan who never once took his eyes off of her. He waved back and looked towards his parents' grave and said "I love you guys, never forget that."

He placed his hands in his pockets as he began to walk off. He felt the sharp edge of a rectangular shaped card and pulled it out. It was Casey's business card. And of course the ink was green.

He strolled back into his office at about, ten after one and he noticed there were some people in his office. "Victoria, what's the deal, why are there people unattended in my office?"

"Sorry Nate, I told them you would back momentarily, they were referred to you."

He looked at her confused. "Referred? Referred by whom?"

She picked up a piece of paper from her notepad and read, "By a Miss. Casey Green Sir."

He took the card out of his pocket and looked at the back, it read, Big Money $$$.

CHAPTER EIGHT

Sorry but Happy Birthday

Tuesday April 3rd, one day before Nathans 28th birthday and he felt like shit. No one in particular made him feel that way, until that morning when his phone rang.

Lately he had been a little stressed out all because of work. If he was going to tackle this case that Casey hooked him up with he would have to do his research and do it well. He also had to get caught up. With missing two weeks and a bit, he had to finish off those cases first, and those that weren't as major as murder, he passed on to other members of them Firm to handle for him.

And as his phone rang bright and early that morning, his heart raced hoping it was nothing but good news or a sweet soft voice of one of heavens angels. "Hi Nathan." It was an Angel alright, it was Angelique. "Yes?"

"I needed to talk to you."

He looked at the calendar and realized the date and he started to laugh, "WOW, two and half weeks later? That has to be some kind of record."

She cleared her throat, "I love you Nate and I need to know that you love me too."

He celebrated in her pain and sorrow and laughed again, "I can't tell you what you want to hear Angelique. You're not and haven't been one of my main focuses right now."

As he flipped through some books digging for some research he could use in his case he heard someone in the background. "Are you in the middle of something? Because I am and if you're done, I'd like to go now."

"Yeah I had a meeting but we had a short intermission type of thing. You're all I think about."

"Now?" He spat at her.

"I'm trying not to cry in front of all these people Nathan, but I can't hold it together any longer."

"Why don't you run up to your hotel room and lock yourself in there? They won't see you or hear you in there."

She started to get upset at his humorous ways. "I need you to be a little understanding."

"Like you were with me? You see, you can't win Angelique."

"I'm sorry Nathan, but for the first time I'm on top and I like being at the top. And yes I was being selfish and I'm sorry, but my intentions weren't to lose you."

"You didn't even fight for me to stay. Just like you didn't fight to move your meeting or do something so you could be there for me. You fought your way to the top though, you showed me where your priorities were Angelique."

"I'll fight for you, okay is that what you want me to say?"

"I'd like it if you meant it." He said as he got up and headed toward his kitchen.

He flung open the microwave and heated up a bagel. "Okay, whatever you want, I'll fight for you."

"My birthday is tomorrow, I doubt you remembered but, I want you here."

After the last words left his mouth his mind immediately focused on Casey. He didn't know whether or not he wanted to say never mind or yell at her and tell her to stay out of his life. All he knew was that it was too late to take it back.

"Oh my gosh, you're going to hate me."

A feel of relief entered his body and he asked her "What is it?"

"I have a photo shoot tomorrow that they just assigned me too."

He laughed again, "Do you Angelique Walters; you've already decided your life doesn't involve me. Do you baby." And he hung up.

He placed his cordless phone back on the receiver in the kitchen and thought to himself. What the hell was I thinking? As much as he loved her and as much as he thought she loved him, did that even mean anything anymore? Should he still even care for her? He always followed his heart and no girl, no matter what they shared, would ever make a fool of him and he would stand by her side. Twice!

That day he took a break from the office. At home he could make his own coffee the way he liked it and he could take a break whenever he wanted to. As the clock hit 11:30am, Nathan pushed the hefty books aside and sat in front of his television and pushed in The Last King of Scotland DVD.

The overall performance of the movie could have him watching that movie all day everyday. He was impressed by Forest Whitaker's role and always dreamed to be as skilled at his job, as Forest was at his.

As soon as the movie ended he made his way back over to his desk. He put his hands over his eyes and leaned back in his leather computer chair. All he was able to wrap his mind around was his trial and that he didn't hear from Casey all day. He didn't remember doing anything wrong, so hopefully she wasn't upset with him or worse, hopefully she hadn't found a man last night at that club she went to. He didn't even know if he wanted to be her man. He didn't know if she wanted him to be her man. Was he really over Angelique the way he believed he was? And was this thing between him and Casey anything to get worked up about? Following his mind and his heart which at that very moment felt the same way about calling her, he picked up his cell phone and dialed her office.

It rang, and went to her voicemail. "Hello, you've reached the desk of Casey Green Manager, Program Director and Head Social Worker of the Dixon & Green Social Corporation. I'm sorry I couldn't get to the phone right now but if you leave me your name, call back number and your concerns and I'll be sure to get back to you as soon as possible. Thanks again and have a great day."

He looked at the clock, it was now four in the afternoon and he felt like his day wouldn't be complete unless they spoke. "Hey Casey, It's me Nathan checking in on you. You have my number and um, I guess my concerns are that…I miss you and want to make sure you're good." He closed his cell phone and threw it on his bed.

For the rest of the day he looked over his books and crammed more and more information into his brain. By 9:45 he was researched out! He still hadn't heard from Casey and he told himself that he wouldn't call her cell phone. He fell asleep and about 12:01am he heard a knock at his door. In only his boxers, he stumbled out of his bed at the sound of the loud knocks and his doorbell. Whoever it was made it seem like it was an emergency, and at midnight, it better be! He flicked on the light switch and swung open his front door.

"Happy Birthday." It was Casey and she brought a bottle of red wine and a huge slice of cherry cheesecake. She put the things down on the side table and hugged his semi naked body. As her chest came into contact with his, her nipples became erect and very obvious. She quickly folded her arms and smiled at him. Nathan closed the door and brought the goodies into the kitchen.

He held Casey's hand and led her into the living room. "Sorry I didn't call you or return your calls. I just wanted to surprise you."

He smiled back at her and said, "You had me worried. But thanks for coming."

She held his hand, "I missed you too."

He remembered the message he left on her answering machine and laughed. Gently, she leaned over and kissed him. And as her tongue massaged his and his lips held hers tightly she took his hands and placed it on her ass as she rose to her knees on his couch and intimately kissed Nathan in celebration of his birthday.

His house phone rang off the hook as well as his cell phone. And she stopped kissing him as he reached for his cell phone. "What are you doing? I was going to turn it off." She took the phone out of his hand and looked at the display screen.

"It's your sister, take it."

He looked at the phone and answered it, "Happy birthday Uncle Nate." "E-V-E!" he exclaimed. As he continued his conversation with his niece, Casey picked up her purse and took Nathans hand as she led him to the front door. "Hold on Evey babe."

He put the phone on mute and kissed her hand. "Thank you for coming. I'm sorry about the call."

"Don't be, and your welcome. I wanted to stop by because I'm gonna be in the office tonight real late. And I decided to make a cheesecake, as another excuse to see you." She blushed and put her coat on.

"I had a craving for cheesecake today believe it or not. And I also had a craving for." His cell phone rang again, and it was his sister calling back.

She laughed and opened the door, "Happy Birthday Mr. Walker. Have fun tonight." He kissed the air as she walked down the steps into her car.

Nathan then picked up the phone. "Who was that?" His sister said to him, on the phone.

"Pardon?"

"You heard me."

He laughed it off, "Thanks for the call sis."

"Mmhmm, have a good one Nate."

Later that day after he stopped in at work he had lunch with the boys. Steven pulled up at the KFC Buffet and Nathan laughed. "How'd you guys know this is where I wanted to go?"

Getting out of the Jag, Gregory answered, "Every man wants his chicken, pussy and a sexy car."

The boys all looked at Gregory as a female walked by when he finished his sentence. She rolled her eyes at him and Shawn spoke, "What about her?"

"Nope! She's a cattie, I could tell. Definitely not a coochie I'd want a piece of."

The boys laughed insanely and walked inside with Gregory trailing in the back. Nathan shouted, "You stay back there bro, you're causing a scene."

It felt good to be around his boys that was for sure. No one ever made him feel that free and full of life. Okay, Casey did. But he needed his boy time and they gave him the satisfaction of being a man, being young, being himself. Not like at work, where they all had to be the utmost professional at all times. Shawn was a Pharmacist, Gregory was an Architect and Steven was an Accountant.

Overall, they were all really accomplished, which is probably why they stayed so close. God knows if one of them had failed, the friendship would have too.

They found a seat and a waitress walked over to them. "Hey, I'm Jesse; I'll be your waitress tonight."

The boys looked up at her and in unison replied, "Damn!" She was truly blessed with a heavenly chest, and a hell of an ass in which they could see, as she faced them at their table.

She looked at them and laughed, "What kind of drinks could I get ya'll today?"

Gregory was quick to respond, "Yes can we get a pitcher of sprite and um, chopped lemons on the side?"

She nodded and said, "Anything else?" Steven and Nathan looked at Shawn; they knew he had something to say, for he hadn't closed his mouth since she arrived.

And he spoke. "It's my man Nates birthday today. Do you guys do anything here for that? Like a free meal or something?" She shook her head no, and blew a bubble with her gum. He leaned over the table a little and using his hand, he beckoned for her to come closer.

"Let's say you give him a lap dance."

Nathan's eyes widen and Steven slapped the table as him and Gregory laughed. She looked flattered and then, Nathan was turned off from her.

"Well, you guys are my last table for the night."

Nathan jumped in, "That will be alright, you can just go home."

"Oh my God, you're gay."

The boys laughed again and Nathan just looked at her, "No, I just don't know where your ass has been. I don't want to catch anything." The boys were mute. Jesse looked at the boys and felt very bashful.

"I'll be back with your sprite."

Gregory quickly responded, "DON'T FORGET THE LEMON SLICES." He turned back and looked at Nathan.

"What?"

"You're an asshole." Gregory said to his friend.

"I don't give a shit, girls like that, you don't want to mess with. She's dangerous."

They laughed at his referral to the Kardinal Official track. And as a group, agreed. Steven suddenly spoke, "But Nate, you could have waited until she brought out our pitcher, now she's gonna spit in it."

Gregory added, "Or at least rub her ass on it."

Nathan smiled.

Nathan decided to stop by Casey's work and surprise her with dinner. She had been so nice to him during the past couple weeks that he hated that she had to work on his birthday.

He entered the Dixon & Green Social Corporation building and called her on his cell phone. "Hey you."

"Hey you? What happened to" and he changed his voice to a girly imitation of Casey. "Casey Greens office, how may I help you?"

She smiled and took off her glasses, "How's the birthday boy doing?"

"Good, I had lunch with the boys at that KFC buffet down the street from my house."

"THE KFC BUFFET! Wow. Very nice, but I guess boys will be boys. Right?"

"Get out of here; we had a hell of a time. If it was you, where would you have taken me?"

She was put on the spot and she had to say the right thing. "Well, I don't know exactly where, but it would be elegantly set by candlelight and some kind of pasta and a light wine." He swung open her office door and shut his cell phone.

"Well I guess I read your mind."

He placed a picnic basket on her desk and took out a bottle of white wine, garlic bread, penne pasta in an Alfredo sauce with minced chicken breast pieces. She looked at him as he took out two wine glasses and four candles. She covered her mouth and couldn't help but laugh as he took out the cheesecake she brought him earlier on that morning.

Casey pushed her chair back and bare footed she walked over to the handsome Shamar Moore look alike that stood over her like a tower. She helped him take out the plates and utensils as he spread a blanket on the floor and took her cushions off of her sofa. They ate and as they ate she couldn't help but smile.

"You didn't have to do this. It's your birthday."

He hadn't been more certain about anything as he was right then at that moment when he said, "I know, and I wanted to spend it with you."

She wiped her mouth and looked at him, "You liiiiike me."

He laughed, "I do, a lot. So um, how was your day?" Nathan jumped in quickly trying to change the subject.

"Uhh, I heard they want to relocate my company in the next four months and I don't want to."

"Oh, that sounds like a good opportunity Case, why don't you take it? Better location right?" ,

She nodded and then put her plate down and moved to the couch and he followed, concerned about her.

"Because, I like you a lot too."

With the utmost serious look on his face he said, "I don't know if I told how much you've changed my life and how much you've brought into my life. But I guess that's why I feel the way I do about you." She rested her head on the palm of her right hand and just watched him as he spoke. "With my mom and everything you've done for me to get through this."

She held his chin and kissed his lips softly. "Don't say anything else babe. I did it because I wanted to."

Nathan answered her, "You did it because you liiiiiike me."

She kneeled down and picked up the plates and all that needed to be thrown out. "Well if I didn't, I wouldn't allow you to distract me tonight, with the amount of work I have to get done." She stopped what she was doing.

"Oh I'm sorry, am I a burden?"

She laughed and pushed him in his solid chest. "No, I'm glad you came. It beats being here by myself."

He put the pasta, the wine and whatever that was left from the garlic bread and packed them neatly back into his basket.

While attending to his basket he asked, "So Miss. Green where's my birthday present?"

He looked over his shoulder and sitting in her black lace bra and matching lace panties was Casey with her cheesecake in her hand.

"Right here."

He turned and faced the half naked Bella in her black Manolos, as she crept over to him with the plate. She spooned out some of the cheesecake and fed it to him. She licked the remainder of the cake off the spoon and uttered, "Mmmm, that's good." He nodded in AMAZEMENT. Coca Cola bottle shape?

Check.

Nathan just stared at her. "I wasn't expecting this." He didn't know where to look first, at her breast that stood at attention or her belly that screamed for attention with that diamond belly ring she had attached to it, or those thighs that hugged and kept the contents in her underwear safe and warm.

His heart began to beat fast, than faster and faster. And as his heart sped up, his penis blew up. She released her hair out of the bun as she hopped up on her desk sitting in front of a stunned Nathan. "Are you sure about this?" Casey bit her bottom lip and nodded.

He unbuttoned his dress shirt and stood there shirtless. She quickly reached for his Prada belt buckle and unfastened it within two seconds. The anxiety build up was evidently too much for Casey to handle.

She kissed and sucked on his bare chest while he lifted her from her desk and moved over to the wall. She wrapped her silky legs around this muscular God as he pressed her forcefully against the wall of her office. Their lips reintroduced themselves and as her feet met the floor, he swiftly unhooked her bra and let those bad boys loose.

Nathan stepped out of his jeans and boxers and once again, picked her up and laid her braless body on the blanket and hovered over her. With a gentle force he entered the wet and heated physique that lay underneath him. "Uhhhhhhh." She let out a sound of satisfaction as soon as the plane met its destination.

After every gentle thrust she'd let out a moan of gratitude. After every rough thrust she'd squirm in every different position her little body knew how. Casey pulled Nathan down to her level and engaged in a kiss that seemed to have knocked all the sense from his head, for Casey easily pinned him down and saddled her man.

"Happy birthday." She whispered as she pumped all she had onto his firm and stiff lower body. Somehow, Nathan found the strength to raise himself to a sitting position while Casey still, went to work on his birthday present. He leaned alongside the couch and held onto Casey and rested his head in her bosom.

Closing his eyes to enjoy the ride, he felt her tensing up, and knew exactly what that meant. Casey cried out in excitement after her climax and breathlessly she couldn't wait for Nathan to reach his peak. "Fuck me Nathan."

He laughed, "Oh, with pleasure baby."

Long slow thrusts in her tight vagina began to drive him to insanity. It had never felt that good, that tight, that wet. And that was it. With her oooing and awing and constant pleads to fuck her and "Faster Nathan Faster" he came and fast at that.

Fulfilled, they laid together naked and sweaty wrapped under the sheets. He ran his fingers through her hair and she caressed his chest with a million and one things to say, but couldn't find the right words.

"What does this mean? Am I a fuck and chuck?"

He laughed, "How old are you and where do you come up with this stuff?"

She joked, "Well I'm a mature 17, don't tell my parents."

He held her tight, "Look at me; you're not a fuck and chuck. I want you, to myself." She closed her eyes out of satisfaction and whispered, "Good. I want you too. Oh and Nathan?"

"Mmhmm?"

"Thanks for distracting me tonight."

CHAPTER NINE

Love To Love You Girl

With the smell of buttermilk pancakes and smoked bacon strips, Nathan woke up with a smile. After carrying a sleeping Casey home with him last night, he slept comfortably knowing that the spot beside him in his bed was no longer cold and vacant.

The smell of her perfume lingered in his sheets and on his pillows. Nathan inhaled and took in all her scents and smiled again. He rose to his feet and followed his belly into the kitchen. The table was set with fresh orange juice, pancakes and bacon. Just as he suspected. But Casey was no where to be found. He checked the front door to see if her shoes were still there, and they were. He walked back into his room and could hear the shower running. Stripping down to nothing, he decided to join his naked lover in the shower.

He pulled open the sliding glass shower door and watched her as she washed her hair. She must have felt the cold air hit her for she turned her head and holding each breast in one hand uttered, "Its cold Nathan, close the door!" He invited himself into the shower and she giggled as he held onto her hips.

"Good Morning!"

"Yes, it is a good morning."

She poured the strawberry kiwi scented body wash all over his chest and rubbed it all over his body. When she moved her hands past his belly button, he jumped.

He rubbed some of the soap off of his chest and splashed it in her face. She washed it off and laughed as she grabbed her towel, he kissed her as she walked out of she shower. As Casey lifted her left leg on the toilet seat to fully dry off her legs, she flushed the toilet. "AHHHHHH." Nathan screamed out.

"Oops! My foot slipped."

He laughed out in the shower. "YOU'RE LUCKY I LIKE YOU."

"Just like?" She flushed the toilet again, 'You better love me." Casey joked with Nathan.

She put one of Nathans t-shirts he had hanging on the back of the bathroom door and walked out of the bathroom. Nathan couldn't even respond all he could do was laugh. After his shower he threw on his boxers and a black wife beater and dried his hair.

He entered the kitchen to see Casey with her head wrapped in a towel and wearing one of his t-shirts which was obviously too big for her. She read the newspaper out loud for her new boo as he poured the syrup over his pancakes and dug in.

As those Aunt Jemima buttermilk pancakes hit his lips he began to realize how good he felt, just sitting there knowing that Casey was right beside him. Felt like a family, minus the fact that they didn't have a child running around the house, or a child squirming in their seat not wanting to eat. He laughed at the thought.

"What's so funny?"

Nathan looked at her and stole a piece of bacon out of her plate and shoved it in his mouth, "Nothing. It was just a distraction." Casey shook her head and put her empty plate in the dishwasher. Nathan finished up his breakfast and followed Casey into his living room where she just sat on the couch.

"You have any video games?"

"Pardon?"

She repeated herself knowing that he heard her. "Do you have any video games?" He walked over to his entertainment center and swung open the door and revealed all of his video game systems. He had everything any child would love to have. It went back to Sega Genesis, Super Nintendo, Nintendo, right up to Wii and XBOX 360.

She walked over and pulled out his Game Cube and put in Mario Kart. She reached for both controllers and handed one to Nathan. "You sure you want to do this?"

"What? Just because I'm a girl means I don't game?"

Nathan took his seat on the couch and replied, "No, I mean you sure you want to face ME in THIS game?"

"Oh yeah, bring it on baby."

She walked back over to the couch and Nathan noticed the smoothness of Casey's ass, as the lace panties she wore, barley covered her bottom.

The game started, they choose their characters and Nathan noticed that she picked Luigi. "Let me guess. You chose Luigi because his clothes are green?"

Casey laughed, "Wow, your smarter than I give you credit for Nate. So let me guess. You chose Wario because you look just like him?"

Enjoying their playful conversation they began the game. After several rounds of racing Casey leaned back. "I whooped your ass."

"Well, you won by default. Two." He said flicking her breasts. "And besides I think I have an ache in my back."

Casey quickly got up and said, "Let me take care of that ache for you." She gently rubbed his shoulders and used all the different hand techniques that she knew how to do.

Enjoying the back rub, Nathan reached for a magazine that he found in Casey's book bag that happened to be lying on the floor beside the couch. "Angelina is pregnant again?"

Casey laughed, "I think it's just a rumor babe, but read it to me, please."

He started to read it, and as he read it to her, they both commented on the pictures and the stories, while Casey continued to rub Nathans shoulders. "Thanks Case that feels a lot better now."

She stopped and laid down across his lap, looking up in his face. "My last relationship lasted five years." her statement caught Nathan a little off guard but still, he continued to listen to her story. "He was an engineer and put himself completely into his work and this was before I even landed my company now, but I just felt so ignored and so..."

Nathan interrupted, "Unimportant?"

She looked at him and he quickly turned his head not wanting her to see the hurt in his eyes from all the damage done by Angelique. "Yeah. I'm only 26 and we broke up when I was 23 and ever since then I was like, forget it. It's not worth it. So, I threw my self into my work, I mean I felt like I was missing something, I didn't understand how it was so easy for him to neglect us for work. And after I decided to take the road he took, when I was 25 I landed the Social Corporation and I neglected guys altogether."

"So what, you didn't go clubbing? You didn't have fun?"

"Oh yeah I did on special occasions, like birthday parties. But as for guys, I wasn't interested."

"He broke your heart?"

She held onto Nathans hand and sighed a miserable sigh, a sigh that indicated that she didn't want to talk about it anymore. "When we were together, I was, let's say desperate for us to work, because we met during our first year in university and I was like what the hell, he was my soul mate. So we tried to get pregnant, and it wasn't until the doctor notified me that I couldn't." She squeezed his hand and continued. "I told him about it and he was disappointed and that's when he decided to completely devote all his waking hours to that company he worked for." She sniffed to clear her sinuses, "I was torn up and I was going through it all by myself." It was instantly that he thought of his situation with Angelique. He wasn't sure which situation was worse but, he knew they were both bad.

"I wish I was there for you Casey."

A single tear ran down her eye. She sat up in his lap and looked into his eyes. "Well, I know if it was you, you wouldn't do that. You'd be there for me and the baby. I don't even think he would have stayed to support the baby. And that's not cool, I don't like guys who run from their responsibilities like that Nate." He nodded in agreement with Casey.

"So have you bumped into him after the break up?"

"Well yeah, he came to my mom's funeral, last May."

Ha! Nathan thought to himself. This excuse of a man found his way to his ex girlfriends mom's funeral and his own fiancé couldn't make the trip. He questioned her, "Alone?" She nodded.

"Yeah, he tried to bring talks about us working it out, but I was already convinced that it was too late for that."

Nathan leaned forward and kissed a very vulnerable Casey. She whispered, "I have to go. My conference is rescheduled for this weekend."

"You're leaving me so soon?"

"Yes I am, I got bills to pay and people I got to please."

She hopped off of him and he replied as she walked into the bedroom, "Yeah, people like ME!" As he slouched in his chair he could see how hurt Casey was, after all he was in her position with someone he cared about.

Casey hollered from the bedroom, "Such a big house for little old you Nate. You even got two spare bedrooms here." He soon got up and walked into his room to put on a pair of jeans.

"I'm a spoiled brat, what can I say. I get what I want. And today, I want you!" She laughed as he kissed her on her neck "Wait!" She said as she pulled her skirt over her waist and pushed him off. "Let's go for a coffee, before I go." Nathan was down, as much time as he could spend with her, he would do it, even if it was only for a coffee. He picked up her book bag and carried it out to his car and they drove to the sit in coffee shop, by her work.

Nathan ordered the drinks and walked back over to the table where another female had joined the group. "Hello?" Nathan spoke, confused about who she was. She extended her left arm out to him to shake his hand.

"I'm Jacqueline."

His hands were full with the Cappuccinos and Casey quickly took them out of his hands. "Nathan." She sat back down and Casey moved over so he could sit across from Jacqueline.

"Jacqueline and I use to work from the same Social Corporation way back before…"

"Before Casey, landed her incredible company. Amazing job Case. You're doing something incredible down there at Dixon & Green."

She blushed a little and Nathan felt like embarrassing her a little bit more. "That's my baby." He kissed her on her forehead. "I'm so proud of her."

Jacqueline awed and then asked, "How long you guys been talking, you look great together."

Before Casey could be honest, Nathan lied. "Forever. I look into those eyes and I lose track of time. Where does it all go?" Casey laughed out loud at how ridiculous he was being.

"I'm sorry, he's extremely immodest." She pinched his cheeks and played along. "But you gotta love him." She giggled and kissed his lips quickly and turned her attention back to her friend. "Jacqueline, how's Jonathan doing?" Jonathan was Jacqueline's fiancé for like ever and Casey was curious to see if they were married yet.

"We finally set a date for the middle of August, and now that you're here in front of me, I'd like you to be apart of it."

"Oh my God a bridesmaid?"

"No, better. Maid of honor."

"Wow big time!" Nathan joked.

Casey pushed Nathan out of the booth and hugged her friend. "Yeah, no doubt. I wouldn't turn that down for nothing." Jacqueline was as happy as Casey was.

"Good! But girl, I've got to run though. Nice meeting you Nathan. I hope to see you there as well."

Nathan joked again, "I wouldn't turn that down for nothing."

He winked at Casey. She watched as Jacqueline walked out and she sat back down, still elated. "Casey, you act as if she just proposed to you and you're the one getting married."

She laughed, "Shut up."

As they drove down to her work, Nathan held onto Casey's hand. She responded to it by rubbing it with her other hand. Then she said, "You'll really come with me to the wedding?"

"Of course I would."

"Don't ever change Nathan."

He pulled up beside her car and put his car in park. "Why do you say that?"

"Because this looks good on you, asshole doesn't." He laughed.

She kissed her index and middle finger and placed it on his lips where he then kissed them back. "I'll talk to you when I get back."

She hopped out of the car, before Nathan could respond with his, I'll miss you. But she knew that he would and he knew she'd miss him. She already did.

CHAPTER TEN

What the %@*$!

A month later and Nathan and Casey were head over heels into one another. When she returned from her conference that weekend, they went out for dinner with Steven and his wife, Nicole.

As Nathan got ready, his door knocked and it was Casey, she wore a short green spaghetti strapped dress. Her hair was in curls and she accessorized with gold.

For her, Nathan wore a green and gold argyle sweater with a black t-shirt inside and black dress pants. As he opened the front door, Nathan was in awe. "Do I know you?"

"Yes, it's your long lost lover."

Nathan leaned over and kissed Casey's glossed lips. She walked in his house and spun around, showing off her new outfit and new hair do. Nathan pulled his lady to him and kissed her again. "I'm so glad my conference is over and I'm back here with you Nate. And we're gonna have fun tonight."

Nathan agreed by spinning around as well and showing off his outfit. She noticed the choice of colour Nathan wore and a huge smile appeared on her face. "You're wearing green." Nathan looked down at his sweater and then looked back at her.

"Yeah, well this girl I like loves the colour. And I knew she'd love me too if I wore it."

She hugged him and then backed off to take it all in. "It looks nice on you, brightens your face and so does that gold chain around your neck, very nice babe."

As Nathan laced up his black loafers, he thanked her for the compliment. "Thank you. And thank you for coming on such short notice."

She laughed and walked outside, "You know that's how I do Nate."

Nathan held onto her hand as he drove, it was almost like a habit of his and Casey commented on it. "I like that you hold my hand when you drive." She rubbed his hand as he held onto hers and smiled.

"I like when you dress like that."

Laughing, Casey pulled down the passenger mirror and reapplied her lip gloss. "Babe, did I tell you how beautiful you look tonight?" She didn't turn her attention from the mirror.

"No you didn't."

They pulled into the parking lot of Le Jardin, an Italian restaurant and Casey turned looking at Nathan who wanted nothing but to kiss her. She put her hand in his face as he leaned towards her, "No Nate, I'm still glossing up."

"Fine."

He headed straight toward her neck and as gently as he could, he kissed and sucked on her neck, tasting nothing but her strongly scented lotion. Casey tried to move as far from him as she could, when she realized how much she was getting into the passion on her neck. "Nathan, behave." She giggled as he wiggled his tongue on her neck, increasing the pleasure and excitement. She squirmed and pushed him off her when his cell phone rang.

Putting her lip gloss in her purse, she watched him as he answered his phone. "Yo, Steve, what's good?"

"Where you guys at?"

Nathan sat up straight and took his car keys out of the ignition. "We're on our way inside the restaurant."

Hanging up the phone Nathan jumped out of the car in a hurry. Casey hopped out too and Nathan hollered, "Get back in that car."

Casey was confused, "What, why?"

"Just get in the car my peppermint."

She sat back in the car and slammed the door shut. He ran over to her side of the car and opened her door. Casey laughed as he stretched his hand out and took hold of hers. "What a gentleman."

They walked into the restaurant. Steven and his wife were waiting out front for them. Nathan hugged both Steven and Nicole and Casey said hello. "Nicole, Steven, this is my lovely Casey Green." Bashfully, Casey shook hands with the married couple and then clung onto Nathans arm as they were escorted into the dining room.

The ambiance of Le Jardin was fabulous. The light fixtures set the mood perfectly to a calming tone, as did the tall scented candles on each table. As well as the center piece which was a miniature bouquet of red and white roses and the music was heavenly sounds of jazz musicians.

As the two couples sat across from one another the conversation began with Nicole's inquiries on how Casey and Nathan met. Casey coughed to clear her throat; she was a little touchy on the subject and didn't know whether or not she should answer. Nathan looked at her as she took a drink from her wine glass. "It's okay babe. We met a few days after my mom and dad died. She was my moms' boss and friend, and um… she needed to know what happened."

As Nicole slowly put her hand over her mouth, everyone at the table knew she regretted the question. "I'm sorry guys."

Casey smiled, "Girl don't be, that's what happened. How else are we going to tell the story, right Nate?" He nodded and drank his wine.

"I must say Casey; I've never seen my man Nate here, so vibrant since his parents past. There was a time when the boys and I never knew if he would make it out of his state. And in bright colors at that."

The table laughed and Nathan shook his head at Stevens' statement. "Me personally, I'm just glad he's okay. Whether or not I got him there doesn't matter."

The Andersons were impressed and Nathan felt very cocky as he witnessed how much they adored Casey. "Oh my God, enough about me and boring Nate over here. How did you two meet?"

Nicole smiled and tackled the question, "Well, my hubby and I have been married for four years and we have a daughter Alexis, who is now two." Casey awed and Nicole continued. "We met at Stevens' job. I went there on the account of business. My boss was in need of an amazing accountant and I met with Steven over it a couple times and what do you know here we are."

Nathan joined the conversation, "So Nicole, what exactly did Steven say to you when you walked into his office." The three of them laughed. Nathan knew exactly what he said and used it four years ago in his best man speech at their wedding.

"What happened?" Casey asked feeling left out.

Nicole replied, "Well I walked into his office and he was on the phone with a client. He motioned with his hands for me to come in and he closed his office door." Steven laughed to himself as his wife continued. "So, he finally gets off the phone and he just looks at me and I said, hi, I'm Nicole Cozier from the Richmond Building down on fifth, and I'm here to take care of business. And he said"

Nathan and Steven both joined in with Nicole and said, "Business, I want to be the only business you take care of." Casey laughed and then awed once again.

"Now I know why you and Nathan are such good friends."

"Why's that?" Steven asked.

"You're both so corny."

"Hey, hey, hey!" Nathan interjected "I am not corny."

"Babe, don't make me embarrass you, right now."

He kissed her hand and winked at her, "Okay I wont."

As they ate, the happy couples talked and got to know one another better. After dinner the waiter returned, "Were you all interested in dessert this evening?"

The ladies both answered, "Yes."

Nathan looked at Steven and they both really had no other choice but to say yes. When their desserts arrived just looking at it made them full. "Excuse me guys, I have to go to the bathroom." Casey excused herself from the table and walked to the washroom.

As she left, Steven commented, "I see your girl is tatted up."

"Pardon?" Nathan questioned.

Nicole laughed and dug into her dessert. "I didn't know Casey had a tattoo."

Nathan was puzzled, "Neither did I."

Steven laughed at his friend and joined his wife while she ate the apple pie and vanilla ice cream, "I'm sure you didn't."

Nathan had not the slightest clue as to what they were talking about, but in the washroom, Casey did.

In the bathroom she realized a very cherry colored, very noticeable hickie on her neck. In shock she grabbed her neck and although no one else was in the bathroom, she was embarrassed. She was mad, she felt like a horny little teenager and she was paranoid about it as she walked back to the table. She had left her make up in Nathans car and with only dessert left, it didn't make sense going to get it to put some on the blemish, just to leave in ten minutes.

She walked back to the table scratching the side of her neck where the hickie lay. As she approached the table all eyes were on her and as she eased past Nathan to her seat he witnessed it too.

He choked on the cheesecake he ordered for her, and also kindly started to eat for her. Steven realized that Nathan saw the mark on Casey's neck and laughed in silence at him. Nathan flung up his middle finger as casually as he could and then put his arm around Casey. She looked at him, like she was going to kill him and then finished her chocolate swirl cheesecake.

As they all stood up to leave, Casey and Nathan trailed behind. Casey whispered, "Baby?"

Nathan responded, "Yes my lovely."

"I have a hickie on my NECK!"

"Yeah, I saw it."

She squeezed his hand, "I hope those guys didn't see it Nate."

He let go of her hand a little and moved closer up to Steven and Nicole. He looked back at Casey and whispered, "They DID!"

Her eyes widened. She felt very uncomfortable at that point. They walked out to the parking lot and they coincidently parked one car apart from each other. Leaning against his car Nathan held Casey close to his chest and rubbed her shoulders as Steven held his wife from behind by her shoulders. "I had fun tonight guys, it was really nice meeting you both." Casey said, slowly getting the hickie off her mind.

Nicole replied, "It was a pleasure meeting you Casey, now I can see why Nathan can't take his mind off of you lately."

"Yeah Casey, no doubt. It's lovely to have you apart of our lives."

Casey looked at Nathan to translate. "He means that me and the boys are so inseparable that it's like we all live life together as one." Nicole laughed, "Trust me girl, these boys will become your best friends."

Casey smiled, "well as long as I have you Nicole, I think I'll be able to handle them."

Nicole nodded and hugged Casey. The boys looked at one another, impressed, satisfied and gave each other props. As the clouds disappeared and darkness fell, the evening came to an end and they went their separate ways.

"Did you really have fun?" Casey reclined the car seat back a little and sighed a sigh of satisfaction.

"Yes sir. It felt good to double date again." She laughed out loud and turned towards her man. "You think, we could be as happy as Steven and Nicole are?"

Nathan turned down the radio and answered her, "It's possible. It's also possible that we could be happier."

"No it's not."

Nathan was alert. He put on his indicator and made the left turn at the top of his street. "What do you mean by that?"

She turned on the light in the car and turned her neck towards it. "You abused my neck. And I'm mad at you; therefore, I'm going home." She hopped out of the car and walked towards her Maserati. "Whoa, hold up. I thought you were going to come in and we were going to... well, you know."

She laughed, "Come here."

Leaning against her car, Nathan walked over to her and kissed her while running his fingers through her silky hair. "That's too bad. I bought the cutest thong for you tonight."

"For me eh?" Nathan laughed.

"Yes, for you." She said snapping the strap against her thigh. 'Too bad you been a bad boy."

She eased him off of her and opened her car door. "So punish me." She hopped in and started her car. As she backed out of his driveway she turned down her window and replied, "I am." She winked then honked as she drove down the street.

Nathan and his boys were hanging out one Sunday before Casey got back from another one of her conferences. "So fellas, I met this girl." Nathan explained to them. Steven made it seem as if he didn't know who he was talking about.

"You mean the girl from your parents' funeral who had the place looking good?" His friend Shawn asked.

Nathan smiled, "Yeah."

As him and his boys chilled on the couch at Nathans house, he thought about and anticipated Casey's return. He anticipated all of her returns; from the bathroom, the shower, from work, her conferences and even from putting him on hold when they spoke on the phone. "So why didn't you tell us about her sooner?" Gregory asked, kind of offended.

"Well, I didn't wanna brag. But me and Casey got it pretty TIGHT!" Steven gave him props, he approved his response.

"So, don't leave us hanging on like that Nate, what's she saying?" Again, Gregory asked after eating the last bit of the chips.

"Well, I'm really diggin' her."

Steven laughed out loud and stated the obvious. "You fucked her didn't you?"

"Fucked is so harsh."

Shawn jumped back in, "So, what, you made love?"

The boys all laughed and Nathan spoke, "Well, call me guilty….. in her office."

The boys all hooted and hollered in excitement, giving him his props and fair share of congratulations. "Well my friend, she was very hot, very proper. I mean dime piece 100%." Gregory stated. The boys all agreed.

"She makes me happy though. She's one of you guys."

As Nathan continued to explain to his friends about his interaction with her the weeks before and when they first met, they were fascinated. Steven had to clown on Nathans 'softer' side.

"Damn Nate, girl had you cooking and setting a picnic and shit?"

"That's serious."

"Get out I stopped at the Pasta Palace on Queens."

At the same time Steven, Shawn and Gregory started to sing Jagged Edge's **Let's get married**. *"Meet me at the alter in your white dress, we ain't getting any younger we might as well do it."* Nathan laughed.

"Could you see you guys making it that far man?" Steven asked after witnessing for himself, how close and happy they were.

"I think it's too soon to say, but on the down low boys." He looked around mysteriously as if someone was there and nodded his head yes. Again, the boys went wild.

Killing the mood, Shawn mentioned Angelique. "So what's good with the promiscuous Angelique?"

Nathan shrugged, "Couldn't tell you bro, I haven't heard from her for a month now, since she flopped me on my birthday."

"Well it's a good thing she flopped." Steven interrupted.

Nathan smiled, "I hear that."

"After the way she burned you at your parents funeral Nate, I don't know how you could even pick up your phone for her anymore. That was just so dishonorable. Any girl ever do that to me, instant lock off!" Shawn commented.

Nathan shook his head in disappointment. He was still really upset about it. "Yo everything happens for a reason boys, if I hadn't been dissed by Angelique the way I did, I wouldn't have met such a phenomenon like Casey. She changed my life for the better."

At that same time they heard a key going into Nathans front door and they all looked towards it, as Nathan got up to see what was going on. The door creaked open and it was Angelique. "Hey boys." The guys ignored her greeting. They were more concerned with why she was there...at all.

"What are you doing here Angelique?" Nathan asked.

"Well if we're going to work on things between us, I figured I should be in the same continent as you, right?"

"Wrong." Nathan rejected her hug. "I thought I made it clear in Europe that we weren't happening ever again if I left."

She looked embarrassed as all the guys watched the confrontation between the two of them. "Well, I had to come back to you Nate."

Shawn yelled out, "WHY? He don't want you."

Steven got defensive and wanted to protect Casey and agreed, "Yeah seriously Angelique, I think you've overstayed your welcome... already."

Angelique looked at them with a dirty look on her face. "I'm pregnant."

Excluding Angelique's, all mouths dropped to the floor. They looked up at Nate as he turned to them and Steven spoke, "or maybe she changed it for the worse!"

Nathan could feel his heart inflate and then within an instant POP! Deflated. Nathan looked at Steven and swallowed hard and began to sweat.

"What do you mean you're pregnant?"

"Do you want me to paint you picture Nathan? I'm having your baby!"

Gregory commented, "You sure, you're not just getting fat?"

Nathan turned to him, he didn't like the humor, this was serious and he was turning it into a joke. The boys silenced. "So you're moving back in here?"

Angelique laughed, "I didn't know I moved out!"

She walked past the boys and into the bedroom. Nathan followed her, and the boys followed Nathan, at a good distance, afraid he may feel them following him. "You kind of did when you gave me back my wedding ring."

"Well give it back to me and I'll put it on."

"You can't be serious. I don't want to marry you. After the shit you put me through."

She stopped unpacking her clothes and sat on the bed. Eating popcorn, the boys stood at the door way and took in the whole conversation. "What did you just say?"

"That's strange. I don't believe I stuttered but, I said I don't want to marry you. So I don't know who you think you are coming back in here demanding attention and a ring. That makes you look really trashy and me personally, I don't like trash."

"Whatever. I don't want the ring, but I'm carrying you're baby and I want us to work. I love you Nate. Why are you acting like this?"

"Tell her, Tell her, Tell her!" The boys cheered and laughed in the hall. Nathan turned around.

"Nathan, look get your groupies up out of my bedroom, I don't like an audience."

"Your sex tape online tells me different." Gregory added as Nathan pushed them out into the hall. It was time for them to leave.

"Fuck you, Greg." She hollered.

"Whatever Freak-a leek. You trifling!"

"Stop it guys." Nathan replied, getting angry.

"She don't love you Nate. She loves that money you're rolling in." Shawn said lacing up his Nikes.

"Well, she's carrying my baby, you seen her little belly. What am I suppose to do?"

Steven intervened, "Well what about Casey. Where does she stand? Or better yet, where does she fall?"

Nathan couldn't even answer him. He didn't even remember about Casey. The boys walked outside and he held his head to the ground! She stood behind him with her hands on her hips. "Tell me what?"

"Nothing." He walked past her.

She shrugged, really she didn't care, she was just one step closer to getting back to what she thought was rightfully hers.

"I can't begin to tell you how good it feels to be back home with you."

"Can't exactly say I feel the same about you being here!" Nathan uttered under his breath!

Chapter Eleven

Sex With You

For the rest of the evening, Nathan was quiet. He went into his room after the boys hurried off and just kept to his self. He knew it was over with Casey, especially since she told him that she didn't like a man who didn't man up to his responsibilities. He hated Angelique now more than ever, but he knew he couldn't hate her 100% after all it was his sperm that made its way to her egg. "Fuck!" He cursed out loud as he got ready for bed.

Angelique walked in the room, "You're not happy about this baby are you?"

"What makes you say that?"

"Well, you didn't even hug me, or congratulate me. That's not the Nathan I left here."

As he read a novel he answered, "I'm just not happy with you. And the Nathan you left here is dead and gone. We've been over this foolishness so many times Angelique, and I'm starting to get sick of it."

She didn't understand what he meant, but she hopped into bed beside him and replied, "Well, you can't say I'm not trying, after all I am here."

He took his eyes off the page and looked over at her. "Try harder honey." He snatched up his pillow and tore the comforter off of her. "What the hell? Where are you going?"

"I'm going to sleep on the couch"

"But the couch gives you a back ache when you sleep on it."

He laughed and turned to look at her, "Well you give me a headache when I sleep with you so, it's a lose lose situation." He walked out of the room and slammed the bedroom door behind him.

She knew her presence there met nothing to Nathan, nothing at all. And she knew that if only she had made it out to be with her fiancé sooner, things would be good. She didn't know how hard she would have to work to get him back, but she hated that she had to.

The next morning she walked out into the living room where Nathan slept. He was wide awake, dressed in a Hugo Boss pine stripped suit with a black dress shirt inside. "Morning Nate."

"Mmhmmm." He sipped his coffee and walked into the kitchen to put his cup in the sink. She hurried in behind him.

"I have a doctor's appointment today, at two. I don't know if you wanted to be there."

"Is this baby mine?"

"YES!" Angelique got very offended.

"So why the hell wouldn't I want to be there? Bout I don't know if you wanted to be there. What the fuck is that?"

She looked like a little puppy that just got shocked or hurt. "I just figured since that you're not talking to me, you didn't want to." He walked over to her in her silk night gown and got on her eye level.

"I'm trying to be nice, by just not talking to you. But don't think you're going to exclude me from this baby Angelique. Now I'll see you two, at two." Throwing in a little humor he patted her stomach and walked off. She looked at him and walked away, "Go the hell to work."

He opened the front door and called out, "What no kiss?" He closed the door quickly just in case she came running or if she wanted to slam the door first. He decided the best bet for that day was for him to focus on his work, his trial and not about Angelique, the baby, or how the hell, he was going to tell Casey when she got back later that day.

The appointment was just an ordinary check up. The doctor pretty much told Angelique the do's and don'ts of her pregnancy and congratulated the two of them. "Your wife is glowing." The doctor commented.

Nathan faked smiled and as his pager went off, he realized it was Casey. "She's not my wife, just some chick I knocked up." Angelique and the doctor both looked at him for his inappropriateness. "Naaaw, I'm just joking. But, seriously believe me when I say she's not my wife." Angelique smiled and quickly interjected, "I'm his fiancé." Luckily for her his phone went off and he didn't get the chance to interrupt with another rude comment. She gave him a dirty look as he walked out of the doctors' office. "Excuse me Doctor Gale."

He walked down the hall a bit and answered his phone. "Hello?"

"Hi, it's me." It was Casey and he felt better.

"How was the conference?"

"Oh God, it was never ending. I got to the office about two hours ago and I'm burnt out as usual."

"Full day ahead of you?"

She let out a long sigh and answered, "Yes, very very long. Where are you?" She heard the intercom go off at the Doctors office.

"I'm at the doctors." He responded without even thinking.

"Is my baby okay?"

His heart numbed when she even uttered the word baby. "You're baby is okay. I'm just with a client, who didn't want to come alone." Dumb answer he thought. She laughed, probably agreeing with him. Nathan quickly tried to change the subject. "Where are you?"

Casey laughed, at what, Nathan didn't know. "I had a short 15 minute break, so I decided to stop by the book store, to pick up a few things for my library at home." She hesitated a little.

"Anything for my library?" Nathan questioned.

"You mean that bookshelf with all your work research texts?" Nathan laughed.

"Maybe I did." Casey said looking at the book she got for him.

She continued to talk as he stressfully inhaled and exhaled. "Okay, babe, I wish I could have lunch with you today, but I can't, I'm booked up until 7:00 tonight."

"Okay, well I'll meet you at Dennys and we'll get some dessert if you want."

"Wow, Nathan you read my mind! I'm having the biggest craving for a cheesecake sundae right now."

He noticed Angelique walk out of the doctors' office and headed down the hall towards him. "Kay Case, I gotta let you go, my clients on his way to me right now and you know."

She interrupted, "You gotta keep it professional, I know. I'll see you at 7:30."

He laughed, "Yeah I'm glad you understand. I'll see you later."

"Nate! … I miss you." She laughed knowing that he couldn't say it back. "Bye" and she hung up on him. As soon as he got down to his car he text her on his I phone, "I miss you too."

Driving back home was painful for the mom-to-be Angelique. She wanted to rejoice in the happiness of becoming a mom and Nathans attitude wouldn't let her. "Who was that on the phone?"

"Oh I'm sorry, but my parents died about two months ago, so who are you to be asking me those kind of questions?"

"The mother of your child." She shot back at him, proud of her response.

"Good answer. But um, unless you're asking me something that has to do with that child, ill answer you. Stay out of my business otherwise."

That shut her up for the rest of the ride home. When he pulled into the driveway he quickly put the car into reverse. "Can I at least ask you what you want for dinner?"

He looked out his side view mirror and responded, "I'll order something when I get back to work." She said okay and got out of the car. As he pulled out, he rolled down his passenger side window and called out to her. She turned and he yelled, "Don't burn down my house!" and sped off down the street.

Through her tears, she fought with her key to fit in the door. As he drove to work, Nathan knew how badly he was treating her and he knew she was probably crying at that point. He just had so much anger built up inside him that he just didn't care.

When he got back to work, he spent the next two hours with his client that Casey introduced him to. As they finished up, the lady asked him, "I'm not trying to pry, but how do you know Casey?"

The question caught him a little off guard and he just accepted it. "Um, she was a friend of my mothers, and when my mother passed away she was a friend of mine. My best friend."

The lady smiled. "She's a beautiful girl, both inside and out."

Nathan rose from his chair, "Yes she is."

He walked his client to the door, "Thank you for coming Mrs. Bennett." She waddled out of the office.

For a lady who looked to be in her late forties, early fifties, she had a derriere that looked like it was holding her back. As she walked it rolled and when Nathan realized how hard he was watching this lady's ass, he closed his door immediately. As soon as he sat down, it was time to go and see his Casey.

He pulled up in a spot and turned off his car and just sat there. Not knowing what to say to her. Should he tell her or should he wait the nine months? No he was being stupid, he couldn't lead her on for so long and he wouldn't lead her on for that long either. It wasn't in his nature to have a girl all about him and him all about her and another woman. He wanted to be all about her and just her, God knows he did. Things just weren't playing out in his favor. And he was confused as to way.

He saw a shadow walk over to his car and he looked out and it was Casey. She had two strawberry cheesecake sundaes in a tray and he was just so surprised to see her that he didn't open the door. "Are you gonna let me in?" she laughed and he quickly opened the door for her.

She got in and he kissed her before she could say anything. He slipped his tongue into her mouth and they made love with their mouths for about ten seconds. He pulled away and said, "I really missed you." She smiled and wiped her lip gloss from off of his top lip. "I missed you so much, I bought you junk food." Casey always told him his diet was terrible and should eat healthier. She knew he wouldn't but it was her way of expressing how much she cared about him.

"Thank you mommy." He felt so dirty. He felt like, he was up to his neck in nothing but shit. And still she looked at him with such grace and excitement in her eyes. It was as if she looked past all that mess.

They ate their sundaes while she told him how her conference went. "They asked me if I had considered moving the company." Nathan swallowed his last bit of cheesecake and looked at Casey for the response. "I told them no, I want to stay here. I have my priorities here that I can't afford to leave behind." She leaned over and kissed him on his cheek in elation.

He knew exactly who she was talking about. Him. He bet himself that she would change her mind and quickly if she found out about the double life he was soon to be living, daddy to Angelique's child and hubby to Casey. Who was he kidding? As soon as Casey found out, his life with her was over. "What's the reason for the move?"

"Well, if I move, the company will no longer be called the Dixon and Green Social Corporation, it'll be the Green Social Corporation."

Nathan was happy for her. "Get out. The owner of her very own company? Check you out; you're the one who's all that and a bag of chips."

She laughed, remembering when she told him that. "This coming from the man who is the top Lawyer at his firm and has been since he was 24? And if I recall, that was only 6 months since you joined the firm."

Nathan shrugged, "I was good, what can I say. But seriously, Casey congratulations, that's amazing." He hugged her and screamed out in excitement.

"Thank you."

"But if you stay."

"Which I am." She interrupted.

"Then what happens to that?"

"Well, then Dixon will relocate."

He nodded and thought about her changing her mind. "You look upset Nate, what's wrong? You don't look happy to see me."

"Are you crazy? Don't ever say that, I'm always happy to see you, Case. I just have a lot on my mind."

"Well, meet me in the back seat and I'll clear your mind of them."

He laughed when she hopped over into the back seat. "It's hot in here." Casey called out.

"Casey, keep your clothes on!"

"Oops."

He turned around quickly to see a fully clothed Casey in the backseat. She laughed, "Come back here. I won't bite you."

He hopped over, "But I want you to."

She put her legs on his lap and lay down. He ran his fingers up her fishnet pantyhose and underneath her skirt. He fit his hand inside her fishnets and she made it easy for him, because she wasn't wearing any panties. He pushed his finger in and out of her vagina and watched her facial expressions change from good to great to even better. She held onto the top of her skirt and began to pull it up. Lucky thing it was short. She unbuttoned her dress top as he helped moisten her insides. She rose to her knees and slipped down her fishnets. As she did that, Nathan prepared for the joyous ride. She climbed on top of him and he entered her with full force. She bounced and she rode the hell out of him. "Did you miss me?" He asked her.

"Yes, yes I did." She moaned as she worked her waist on his stiffness.

"How much did you miss me?" He whispered in her ear.

"A lot." She panted.

He sucked on her neck and she called out in pain. He stopped, smiled and looked at her bounce up and down on his lap and he was in heaven. Suddenly, Trey Songs, Last Time played on Casey's phone as her ring tone and she just let it ring. After taking in the lyrics, he began to feel like a jerk. His dick quickly became limp. And Casey could tell.

"What's the matter? Is it me?"

"No, I'm just having a shitty day. God! I'm sorry I didn't want to do this to you, I just have a really big case that is taking all of my energy since you been gone. I'm just stressed!"

"Oh." She was convinced and can't say she wasn't disappointed though.

As she pulled back up her pantyhose she said, "Oh I thought my sex was whack or something."

Nathan looked at her, "No baby, sex with you amazing. I get shivers just thinking about it. Don't ever ever feel that way."

She shyly nodded. "Come here." She fell into his arms and he kissed her on her forehead. Still all he could hear was Trey Songs Last Time. *'Yep this is the last time I'm all caught up and it's time to put it down. You really got me trippin, hold up baby girl just listen, this is the last time.'*

Tanya was in town on a business trip with her husband, when she found out that Angelique was not only back, but carrying her brothers' child. "What the fuck?" was the first thing out of her mouth, the Sunday morning that she arrived. She sat across from Nathan as he poured himself another cup of coffee to drown his understandable pain in. Devon looked over at his brother in law as he witnessed the stress he was suffering, as his hands could not keep still.

"What are you thinking about?" he asked.

"I want my mommy and daddy." Nathan joked.

They smiled and Tanya let out a loud sigh and Nathan quickly replied.

"I am thinking about how much I am going to hurt Casey."

"Yeah but this wasn't your fault. Okay, well I mean TECHNICALLY it was, I mean you definitely should have strapped up little bro. I mean this is Angelique, only God knows what she could have."

Devon nudged his wife under the counter and she stopped and apologized.

Nathan laughed, "Is this your way of helping? Seriously, God, my life is so fucked!" Nathan threw his hands on his head and pulled back his hair.

Devon looked at Tanya, for her to extend some sympathy towards her brother, who needed that more then he needed another cup of coffee, which he again, reached for.

She got up out of her seat and hugged her brother, "Don't worry baby brother, Jesus loves you." Again he laughed and pushed her off, "Okayyyy, we do too. Come Devon, group hug babe." Devon stood up and hugged his wife and brother-in law and laughed. They all realized how the presence of family was critical in getting over a loss or stressful times in ones life. And it is. When family or people you really love and treasure are around, you can't see what is wrong, only what is right. Subtract oneself from that equation and all those stressors return, but with family involvement, it makes rough times, smoother than they actually are.

Interrupting that family moment, the front door swung open and laughter flooded the air, a female laugh and a male laugh. Tanya quickly exited the kitchen and walked to the front door. Angelique spoke, "Oh my gosh Tanya, how are you!?" Tanya looked at her, in disgust. How could she pretend like she didn't know, and life was good, when she ruined pretty much everything in her brothers life. She wasn't concerned as to what she had done to her, because Angelique had no control over her life, but she did care about how she dealt with her brother.

Ignoring the question she asked her own, "Who is this?"

The guy reached over towards Tanya, "Michael, I'm Angelique's boss at Lady Magazine."

"Hmm, I'm Tanya, Angelique's baby daddy's sister." Angelique looked at her in disgust as Michael smiled and looked at Angelique. Tanya cursed Angelique with her eyes and called out to Nathan, who was just finishing up on a call.

"Nathan, nice to meet you, Michael." he reached his arm forward again, for another hand shake.

"Ohhh, new boss right? Yeah I heard some stuff about you. How was Europe?"

"Great, I'm actually on a temporary leave for a few days, my wife just had a baby and I couldn't miss it."

Tanya laughed out loud and held onto Devon who then joined the conversation. Nathan looked at his sister, knowing she was about to snap. "Funny, because our parents died a few months back and um, Angelique couldn't leave for this family emergency when it happened. So you're her boss, care to explain why she couldn't leave Mike?" Devon held onto his wifes shoulders, he knew when she was about to get upset. And this was it. Michael looked as though he was a little caught off guard. "I'm sorry; I didn't know anything about that. But I assure you, if Angelique had noted to me that it was a family emergency, she would have been granted leave.' He turned to Angelique and asked her, 'Who did you ask for leave Angelique?"

Four sets of eyes all peered into her skin, demanding an answer, the truth and hopefully the right answer. She couldn't answer. Nathan felt bad for her and interrupted her before she answered. "Forget it. Why does it even matter who she asked. It doesn't change the fact that she wasn't there. She didn't want to be there, she had her priorities at a job, that obviously wasn't so important because she quit it as soon as she found out she was pregnant. Spare yourself the embarrassment Angelique and don't answer."

"Wait a second Nate. If she quit her job, what are you doing here?"

Angelique replied, "He's here because he wants me to start working from home. I'm such an asset to the company that they needed me back."

"Oh wowwwwwwwwwwww!" Tanya exaggerated, "Another joke, you're such an ass to this family, we didn't need or want you back, but somehow here you are. You're lucky my brother is a lot more like my mother and not like me who is more like my father, Jeffery Walker because if it was me, baby or no baby, the day my parents died would be the last part of my life you ruined!" Another awkward moment passed and Nathan could see and feel the shame in Angelique's face, but he didn't even feel like defending her, but still he did. "Tanya, it's okay, Jesus loves her."

Michael spoke, "Jeffery Walker is your father?" They looked at him and Nathan nodded. "I worked with him, he's an amazing accountant. I tried to get him to join the company 2 years ago, but he said due to his family he couldn't."

Tanya looked at Nathan, "What does that mean?" Nathan shrugged.

As he walked his sister and Devon to their car, he sighed aloud and hugged his sister. "I'll be okay guy, stop worrying about me." She looked up at him and said, "I'm worried about Casey. I'm worried that she'll misunderstand your character and why you're doing what you're doing. I'm also worried because what if this is a mistake. Like I understand that she's pregnant, but what if you two, aren't meant to be together?"

Chapter Twelve

The Day We Became Me

Within the blink of an eye, Nathans parents died. Within a blink of an eye Nathan saw that his Angel wasn't an Angel. Within a blink of an eye Nathans life significantly improved when he met Casey. And within a blink of an eye, that relationship would be destroyed.

For the next three days after she came back from her conference they talked everyday. They had conversations while they were both at work and they even had lunch together on the Wednesday. Every time he saw her, she was always glowing; she never had a dull moment. As they finished their lunch he had to tell her one last time how much she meant to him. "I can't begin to explain to you, how much I cherish our relationship. I respect you with all my heart and I would never hurt you intentionally for you've been nothing but careful and gracious with my wounded heart."

As he held her, she looked up at him and nodded, "I know you wouldn't." He kissed her forehead and held onto her even tighter than before. He hoped that him saying that would ease the pain when he finally told her the predicament he was in, knowing that any intention wasn't there. At that very moment, he felt it was appropriate to cry. He was holding onto the one thing that he cared for so much, that he would soon have no other choice than to let her go.

The next day around lunch time, Nathan decided to stop in at Casey's office when he got there she was finishing a phone call so he waited outside. "Oh my God, I knew it! Thank you so much, you don't know how happy that makes me! We'll be in touch." She hung up the phone and she was ecstatic.

She finished wrapping the book she bought for Nathan and she wrote To My Nathan. As she finished writing his name he walked into her office, startling her, she shoved the book in a box under her desk that held all the things from his mothers' desk. She hopped out of her seat and ran over to Nathan, grabbed his face and kissed him. As his eyes rolled back in his head as he was intertwined in all the romance that kiss brought he pulled away. "Just the man I wanted to see." She still smiled so brightly.

She knew in her heart that something was wrong with him by the look on his face. "What's wrong Nathan?" He struggled to find the words.

"Um, I don't know how to tell you this without it hurting you." Casey's stomach bubbled as she could feel this was going to be bad.

"Oh God, it's gonna be bad isn't it?" He nodded. She backed off and sat at the edge of her desk and sighed out loud. "Okay, it's okay. I'm sure whatever it is, we'll be able to work through it together." She smiled and he felt like jumping the hell out of the window and ending his life. He came there to break her heart and she still had such belief and hope in him.

"Kay Casey, there isn't any right words in the English language to make this seem any better than it is."

She fixed the sweater to cover her shoulders and through her fears she laughed. "Nathan can you just tell me what's wrong with you so I can tell you what's so right with me?"

Before even thinking about it he blurted out, "My fiancé is back in town and she's pregnant."

Slowly, Casey's eyes widened and she took her eyes off of him. "I didn't know you were engaged."

"Well I wasn't when we were talking Casey. Oh God. It sounds really bad I know. But I was engaged before you and I met."

"So you cheated on her?"

"NO!" he was very defensive. "I would never do that to her or you."

She shot a dirty look his way and replied, "So what is it?"

"We were engaged and when my parents passed on she couldn't find time in her busy schedule for me and my feelings and she wasn't there for me at that time in my life. And I felt really annoyed and really disrespected and I flew out to see her after. And that's when she gave me back my ring and said we needed time apart."

She turned her head away because she didn't want to believe him but her heart already did. "I had no intentions of getting back with her whenever she came back home Casey you have to believe me. It was over! She showed me that I couldn't marry someone who wouldn't show a little sympathy at a time like that."

He stopped and walked closer to her. "I want to be with you not her. I need you to trust me on that."

"Don't touch me!" She slapped his hand as it reached for hers and she walked over to her seat. "Trust you? I couldn't even trust you enough for you to tell me you were engaged. That wasn't something you found important to share?"

"I didn't want to bring it up, I was still healing in so many ways."

"SO YOU LIED TO ME NATHAN!?"

"NO I Care about you Casey. God I Love you."

She shook her head as her eyes filled with tears. "You don't mean that! You led me on since I came back. That's what was wrong with you wasn't it? It wasn't only your case! Hell, it probably had nothing to do with your case!" She realized something as she spoke. "That's who you were at the doctors' office with, WASN'T IT?"

His silence clarified that for her. Her office phone started ringing. "Look, I'm sorry. Her coming back was so unexpected. You need to understand."

"You need to get out of my office."

Nathan stood there as if he had more to say to her. "I said get the hell out of my office Nathan!" He turned to leave and she slammed the door as soon as he left. Casey screamed out loud to herself and walked over to the couch where they made love and sat down. She folded her arms and just cried as the phone rang and rang and rang.

Nathan got back to work and called his best friend Steven on the phone.

"Yo what's up Nate?"

"Nothing, I just got back from Casey's."

Steven realized what was at stake for Nathan. "Oh yeah, how'd she take it?"

Nathan laughed at such a stupid question. "How would you take it?"

"Oh, my bad Nate. I don't know what to say. No one saw this coming you know?"

Nathan sighed in agreement, "Yeah especially me."

"Well Nate, just say it wasn't you." Steven laughed trying to lighten the mood. Nathan nodded as Victoria walked in to let him know his 2:30 appointment was there.

"Yeah I wish it wasn't." Shortly after, Nathan cut the conversation off and attended to his 2:30 appointment.

Later on that night Nathan went home to Angelique, who immediately started nagging him. "Nathan, my strawberry kiwi shampoo is done. How can it be finished?"

Nathan laughed remembering when Casey was over and that she used it. He then shrugged and walked into the kitchen. She followed and continued, "God Nate, what am I suppose to use now that it's done and I need to wash my hair!"

"WOMAN PLEASE! Can I breathe for two seconds before your attacks? Here, here's ten dollars, go buy a new one." She snatched the ten dollars out of his hand and kissed him on his cheek. She skipped out of the kitchen and as soon as she did he wiped his cheek in embarrassment.

As soon as she left he walked over to the fridge and pulled out a bowl of Angelique's fruit salad. He looked at the bowl and said to himself, "Yeah right." Shoving the bowl back into the fridge he thought about Casey.

Nathan had called her all day and it just kept ringing. It got to the point where she forwarded her calls to her secretary before they got to her. One time the secretary answered and asked if he wanted to leave a message, Nathan agreed and said, "Yeah, can you tell her that Nathan called." He knew deep down in his heart that she wouldn't call back, but he tried. After Nathan changed his clothes he sat on his bed and noticed Angelique left her precious berry on the night table. He picked it up and called Casey. She was ignoring his phone calls but she would have to answer it if she didn't recognize the number. "Casey Green."

"Hi." She recognized his voice, and still it gave her butterflies. "What can I do for you Nathan?"

He stuttered, "I didn't plan on taking up too much of your time." She snapped back, "So don't!" It hurt her to be rude to him but she had to, it was her only defense.

He lowered his head and threw himself back on his bed. "I deserve that." She sighed indicating that she wanted to get off the phone. "Um, I just wanted to say that you gave me what Angelique couldn't and that doesn't mean for a second my feelings for you has changed." She heard him call her name and looked at her phone and saw Angelique Walters on her caller display. She put her hand on her head as she continued to stress over it. "I just hope you understand that I'm doing this because I have to, not that I want to." Selfishly she hated herself, because if she didn't make such a big deal about not liking guys who didn't stand up for their responsibilities, he would still be hers.

"Take care of your family and just forget about me." And before he could respond, she hung up. He erased the number and put the berry back on the night table and just laid there. "Fuck." He said to himself.

For the next two weeks Casey Green changed her life around. She started off by changing her cell phone number so he couldn't call her, and listed it as a private number. She buried herself in her work and created new workshops on different issues like teenage pregnancy and drug abuse and it's effects on the family. Casey tried her hardest not to have time to think about Nathan or what they had together. When her last relationship failed she was all about work and when she met Nathan she vowed to live life and stop living at work because Nathan was now apart of her life that she didn't want to neglect. And now that he wasn't going to be apart of her life anymore, it didn't matter how many hours she devoted to the company because every hour would never be wasted. For two weeks she avoided Nathan as best she could. Whenever he showed up her secretary would say, "I'm sorry Miss.

Green is in a managers meeting" or "Miss. Green is with a client." Shortly after he left she would walk into Casey's office. "Hey Casey, It was Nathan again." She would just nod and pretend like it didn't affect her in front of Tracy her secretary. But it did. And when Tracy left for the day, so did she. She didn't want to get caught there by herself and have him show up because she knew herself too well. For most of the week, Casey worked from home. She would only come in when she had client appointments. Casey knew if she didn't change up her work life style and Nathan showed up, she would do something with him that she would regret.

It was weird. Within the blink of an eye her life changed the day Nathan walked into her office. And within a blink of an eye her life changed the day he walked out of her office.

CHAPTER THIRTEEN

After All Is Said And Done

Casey walked up the steps of Nathans house with a box of his mothers' things from work. Evelyn had left some things on her desk that Casey felt needed to be brought to her son for if she hadn't, she would forever be reminded of him. She even included a picture of her and Evelyn that she took off of her desk to give to Nathan as a present.

She didn't see his car in the driveway so she called him to check in to see if anyone was home. No answer. She figured his fiancé would be home and she continued up the steps. She knocked the door and Angelique answered. Casey was shocked, she was so pretty. She suddenly figured that Nathan lied when he said that he didn't want to have anything to do with Angelique, why not, she was beautiful. "Hi, I'm Casey. I use to work with Evelyn, Nathans mom and I have some stuff that I told him I would bring by."

She smiled at Casey and replied stretching out her hand. "Hi, I'm Angelique. That was nice of you." She put the box on the side table and looked at Casey. "I'm sorry Nathan isn't here to thank you himself, he's in court today, and he had this really big case that he says his best friend introduced him to." Casey smiled knowing that he was talking about her.

As Angelique's cell phone rang, she said, "I should go now." "Hey baby hold up one sec. Well it was a pleasure meeting you Casey. I'll be sure to tell Nate you stopped by." Casey nodded and walked down the steps. That was weird. Why didn't she just tell him right then that she was there, after all she seemed as if it was him who called.

As she got back into her car she dialed his number. "Nathan Walker, talk to me."

"Hi Nate." He was surprised.

"Casey? Wow. You wouldn't believe where I am right now."

"On your way home?"

"No not quite, I literally just finished winning my case with the Bennett's. I'm stepping out of the court room right now." Casey took his word for it; she knew he wasn't allowed to have phone calls in the court room.

She fumbled with her words and then managed to say, "You talk to Angelique today?"

The question caught Nathan off guard, "Um, since I left the house this morning no. Why?" Casey thought to herself, what the hell? "Nothing, I uhh, dropped your moms stuff off for you and I was just calling you to tell you that, I dropped it off."

He had a brief conversation with the Bennett's and she heard Mrs. Bennett say, "Thank you so much Nathan, really. And Casey that lovely lady of yours is truly lucky to have someone like you she can call a friend."

They both felt like shit, him more than her. He then dismissed his client and said, "Thank you. Very kind words Mrs. Bennett, but we will reconvene on Monday morning. You guys take care and drive safe." The family laughed and Casey smiled to herself at what a gentleman he was. "Sorry about that Casey."

"No problem, you've done worse to me."

"Sorry about that too."

Nathan responded almost instantly, knowing that, that response would follow his apology.

"Mmhmm."

She heard his car door slam. "Well, I'm going to let you go."

"Casey?"

She stopped him before he could continue, "Don't. Please just don't Nate."

They said their goodbyes and they hung up. Casey couldn't help but think who Angelique was talking to. She shrugged her shoulders and continued on about her own business. She had her own shit to deal with. Angelique didn't care about her, didn't even know her. Her business was none of hers unless she was her client and she wasn't. Casey wanted to turn the Casey and Nathan chapter in her life. So she flipped that page.

That night, Nathan met up with Steven at a bar. It had been only a week since he told Casey the truth and although apart of him should be happy with the blessing he was going to receive in a few months. He just wasn't. It was almost as if, his parents died, all over again and this time, he was the one holding the gun and pulling the trigger. "Drowning all your troubles down with, Alizé my man?" Steven spoke over Nathans shoulder.

"Yup."

"That's a ladies drink Nate." Steven pulled up the stool beside him.

"It was Casey's favorite drink."

Steven nodded in understanding as he remembered her order at the restaurant. He then ordered himself a Heineken.

"She went to my house today, to drop off some of my moms things and Angelique was there."

Steven commented, "That had to hurt her." Sipping the Alizé, Nathan nodded a slow and regretful nod. "I hate to see you like this Nathan, you look terrible."

Nathan laughed a rough and still heart broken laugh, "Can things be any worse? I left my other half, for a chick who my parents warned me about. Casey was my left, and I was her right. She was my up and I was her down. Within 2 and a half months, we built something better than the two and a half years Angelique and I existed." He finished his drink and ordered Vodka, straight.

Steven looked at him and touched his shoulder, "I'm here for you man. Don't let Angelique get the best of you. You're better than that. If you and Casey are meant to be together, let no man tear that apart. How many times have you said that to me, when it came to Nicole?" Nathan nodded slowly to himself in agreement. "Gods not the only one up there looking out for you Nate. Have faith. Besides, fate is what brought you two together in the first place."

CHAPTER FOURTEEN

Can I Stay With You?

Nathan woke up bright and early Monday morning. The night before the boys were over and they secretly held conversations about Casey and watched the football game, while Angelique catered to them and their every need.

Nathan didn't want her to but the boys were convinced that she owed him for missing the funeral. He loved hanging out with them because, they made it through some pretty rough shit, but still they stayed a group of educated black men who had each others back. Like Casey, and like Angelique did they made Nathan feel like his life was worth living.

As he got ready for work that morning he remembered the night before when Gregory said to Angelique in response to her saying, "What else can I do for you boys?" "You know what you could have done for my man Nate Angelique. Swallow some of dem birth control pills." The boys all laughed and Nathan couldn't help but laugh too. His friends only started to be cruel to Angelique, now that she royally messed up. And she hated it.

He remembered that when she spoke early that morning, "I have an appointment on Wednesday at two. So I don't know if you even want to be a part of this pregnancy."

He looked at her, "You know I do."

"Your friends don't seem to think so."

"My friends aren't in my heart."

She eased up a little bit and sat on the stool beside him. "I want to be in your heart."

"I'm sure you do."

He hopped off the stool and grabbed his brief case from the bedroom. Angelique's black berry went off and he answered it. "Michael my man. Hold on let me get your sunshine."

She ran in the room and looked vex. "Michael, I'll call you back." Nathan sat down for this. "What did I say about touching my blackberry?"

Nathan got up and laughed, "Actually nothing. But I'm assuming by your tone, that you don't want me to touch it. Right?"

"Yes Nathan! I don't answer your phone or touch anything you don't want me to. Shit! It's the only thing I have in this house."

"Yes because this isn't your house remember? It's mine! And don't gimmie that shit, you answered my door the other day, did you not?"

She put her hands on her hips. "What! Was I not supposed to see the fucking books and pictures your mom left at her office?"

Nathan shook off his anger and said, "I honestly think this baby thing will work better, if you lived by yourself with your baby. You don't even do shit when you're here."

"Well I quit my job for you!"

"For me!? Who the hell told you to do that? As a matter of fact, go call Michael and ask him if you can live with him. He still works I'm sure."

She snapped, "He's still somewhere in Europe."

Nathan opened the front door, "So move there!" and slammed it behind him.

Arriving at work the Bennett's were already there awaiting his arrival. They handed him an envelope and a bamboo plant. "You didn't have to do that."

Mr. Bennett replied, "No Nathan, we wanted to."

Mrs. Bennett jumped in. "This plant means love and happiness to come in the near future."

At that same moment Casey walked in with a bottle of champagne and balloons that said congratulations. His face started to glow and his heart started to race. "We all know that Nathan needs some love and happiness right about now." She winked at him and the Bennett's stood up to hug and thank her.

Shortly after the Bennett's left, she put the champagne on his desk. She tied the balloons to his chair and hugged him. "I missed you Nathan Walker." That statement totally had him bewildered. And he smelled her hair. She stood back and he looked at her in dress shorts with her flat ballerina slippers and with a black and gold tank top. "You cut your hair."

She roughed up her hair a little and nodded with a smile, "Yeah, your mom always told me I'd look cute with short hair, so I decided to give it a try." She sat in the chair across from his and Nathan sat back down.

"I had a dream about my mom last night."

"Oh really what about?"

He looked up to the sky and smiled, "She said congratulations and that she's proud of me."

She avoided eye contact. "Sounds like something she'd say."

She looked around and then stood up to close his office door. "So open up that cheque. Show me the money!" He laughed and she hid all her feelings behind her smile. He opened the envelope and showed her the five thousand dollar cheque.

"Well Mr. Walker, big money."

He got up and hugged her. They pulled apart and they looked at each other and for a second, everything that happened between them, faded and all that mattered was how they felt about each other. Right then. They met each other at the half way point of a kiss and they kissed in the middle of Nathans office, until Victoria opened the door and cleared her throat.

"Victoria?' He knocked on his desk and then replied, "Try that." She knocked on the door and he said "Yes now next time can you do that for me?"

She nodded, "I'm sorry, you have a call on line two."

"Thanks Victoria."

She looked at Casey and fake smiled. She hated to see her all over her fine boss, and like many girls unfortunately do, she envied her because she was successful and got the good man.

Nathan walked over to the phone and took the call, it was his sister. "Tanya, can I seriously call you back, in like, an hour?"

"Nate, it'll only take five minutes." She assured him.

His sister just quickly informed him about the information from his parents' insurance papers and everything else that they put off at the time of the funeral. While he was on the phone with his sister, Casey was writing something down on a piece of paper. Nathan quickly ended the conversation with Tanya and he walked back over to Casey slowly, not knowing if she would want to continue or if she would realize what they were doing and stop them.

As he approached her she handed him the paper. "My new place. Meet me there in ten minutes." He was in total shock. What made her want to have anything to do with him was beyond him, but he sure as hell wasn't going to turn her offer down. He had more sense than that!

He pulled up to her house and admired it before knocking on the door. As soon as he knocked she opened it. Nathan didn't know if she was being kind, or if Casey was really happy to see him. After all, she did invite him there.

In her living room she had a collage of pictures of herself and he commented. "You model?" She handed him a glass of champagne.

"Well, I did when I was with my ex. Just something I did in my spare time when he wasn't around."

"There are a lot of shots."

She laughed "Yeah well, he was never around."

They sat in her living room and he sipped his champagne. "No really, these are really nice shots. Is that you're birthmark?" He noticed a light patch of skin on her belly.

She was self conscious. "Yeah, you just never noticed it, because, well, you never seen my bare belly in the light."

Nathan felt uncomfortable, he didn't want to talk about their sexual history, and he didn't think it was appropriate. But maybe Casey didn't have a problem with it. She laughed, "Nathan, we had sex a couple of times, don't be so self conscious. It was never really daylight for our scars and blemishes to show you know?" Nathan wasn't sure if she was talking about the scars in their lives or the scars on their skin.

As she explained her self, he could tell that she wanted nothing else but to have sex with him again. He could always tell, she would get this look on her face; she would distance her self from him as far as possible and avoid eye contact. And that's what she was doing. She always told him, how sexy he was when he just stared at her. It made her feel sexy and him desirable.

"The pictures are very beautiful. I really like the presentation of it." She sipped her champagne and nodded. "Thank you."

Staying calm and cool Nathan complimented her home. "Very nice place." She sipped her champagne and thanked him again.

"Come let me give you a tour." She led him throughout the lower level of her house and then led him upstairs to the bathroom, her live in office , her library and then of course, the master bedroom.

He kicked off his shoes and jumped in her bed. She got worried, "A pet peeve of mine Nate is a messy bed." He flipped over her all black duvet cover and went underneath it.

"Oh God it's so warm underneath here." He exclaimed.

"Get out of my bed Nathan!"

Nathan pretended to be sleeping by snoring and Casey soon climbed into the bed and put the pillow over his head. He over powered her and grabbed for a pillow. Hitting each other back and fourth they laughed and fooled around for a while until Casey hollered, "I SURRENDER! Don't hit me no more. You're messing up my hair!"

"Say you'll be my slave and love me endlessly."

She looked him in his eye, "I will love you endlessly, no matter who you're with." He could tell how serious she was and they began to kiss.

As they kissed she removed his shirt and then removed hers. Quickly they both slipped out of their bottoms and proceeded with their love making. In their time of ecstasy and romance, they forgot all about who was pregnant, whose heart was broken and who lied to whom. It wasn't time for that. It was a time for slow and calm love making between them. Both who lost the same amount of things, who gained the same amount of things and who experienced things that only soul mates would experience. They understood each other and obviously they were inseparable. Nothing else mattered when they met.

Claiming his territory, Nathan noticed how Casey demanded this sexual satisfaction from him. But it wasn't just about sex with them. It was about intimacy and friendship and this strong understanding that they had between each other. As their afternoon of passion came to a satisfying and spectacular end they laid there and Nathan held onto Casey as tight as he possibly could.

"What time do you have to get back to the office?"

He immediately responded, "I don't want to go back, I want to stay with you. Forever."

Casey snapped back into reality after he said that. "You're the only one that knows what I go through on a day to day basis." He made circular motions in the palm of her hand and gently kissed her lips. They felt so right.

You always hear how can something so right be so wrong and never know what it means until you yourself are in the situation. Although it felt so right, they both knew that once they put their clothes back on, all their chemistry and passion was impossible to persist. They needed a miracle to save them. Casey rose up on her elbows and looked at Nathan as he lay there with his eyes closed.

"You thinking about the baby?"

"I'm thinking about having a baby with you."

She knew he was thinking about the baby, but she played it off because he always put her first. "You don't have to lie, I won't be offended."

He opened his eyes, "I'm still having a hard time believing it. It was so out of the blue. Like I'm trying to figure out when we even had the time to make that baby." Casey's house phone rang and it was Tracy from the office.

"Hey Casey, sorry to bother you at home, but I realized your cell phone was off, and your one thirty appointment is here."

"Oh shit. I forgot about her. Kay, I'll be in give me 15 minutes."

And she hung up the phone. "I should go." Nathan stated. She didn't want him to go. She wanted him to stay with her, but she knew that wasn't possible. They got dressed and walked outside together. "You going home to…"

"Cruella Deville? Yes, yes I am."

She held onto his shoulders as they stood in her drive way and laughed at his joke. "I think you should try to make this work between you and her." He looked around the neighborhood and couldn't believe what he's hearing.

"You're being serious?" She shook her head yes. "Why?"

"I don't know, you guys had something first."

"Why do you care about her? You think she gives a damn about anyone but herself?"

She held onto his hand, "Just like you're not giving one about anyone but yourself?"

"I am though, I'm thinking about you."

'What about the baby? Your baby?"

"You are my baby."

She was about to tear up but she stopped her self. "I have to go Nate. I think its best we focus on what our lives have in store for us…separately. Oh and I've accepted the job offer and we move in September."

She hopped in her car and left. Nathan was just so confused. His mouth didn't have enough strength to even respond back to her. He just froze on the spot like he did back in February when his parents were murdered. They just made love and everything between them was great. What life was he living just then? Satisfied but yet at the same time disappointed, Nathan drove home to Angelique. For the sake of Casey, he would give them a try.

He walked in the door and proceeded with caution. Angelique was on her blackberry laying in the bed giggling. She didn't even notice Nathan walked in. "Can you get off the phone we need to have a serious talk." He frightened her and she held her heart.

"Don't do that Nathan." She got off the phone and then began to speak. "I um, tried calling some of the girls so that I could stay with them, but they haven't come in from work yet. So I'll try them at around six."

He took off his blazer and sat beside her on the bed. Taking in a deep breath he calmly spoke, "I don't want you to leave. I want you to stay here so we can work on me and you, so that when the baby comes we'll be okay."

She hugged him. "You mean that?"

He peacefully answered, "Yes, I mean that."

She grabbed his face out of excitement and kissed him and he kissed her back. For a split second he was kissing the old Angelique that he was in love with not too long ago. He pulled away not even realizing what he was doing. Before he could speak she put her finger over his lips and told him to shhh.

"I know you hate me and you've hated me for so long, but really I am so sorry I hurt you the way I did. Everyday when I sit here alone I realize how much you loved me and how much you did for me and I didn't even try to be there for you Nate and I'm sorry for disappointing you."

"Thank you, I'm finally at ease with you. All you had to do was say it Angel."

"Wow, you just called me Angel.' Her blushing made him smile. 'Well I wont disappoint you again Nate."

"That's good to hear. Well, I'm going to take a shower."

"Can I come?"

He looked back at an innocent Angelique and his heart said no, don't let her in too soon, but his mind said you never know until you try. He nodded and she ran behind him and jumped on his back.

After taking the shower, they laid in bed watching The House of Payne by Tyler Perry on Peachtree T.V. Angelique moved closer to Nathan and he put his arm around her. Holding onto her, holding onto the possibilities of making this work, he then thought, 'how could something this wrong be right?'

The next week, Nathan found himself going over to Angelique's parents' house for dinner in celebration of the new baby. He thought it was a little too soon for celebration, but then again, anytime is time for a baby celebration. As they got into Angelique's Porsche, the drive was silent. Neither of them knew what to say, were they together again? Or were they just pretending to want to be with each other. Angelique knew that she wanted to be with Nathan, now she was sure of that. She wasn't before which is why she let him go, but she convinced herself and even tried with Nathan, to express how much she really did want to be with him. He was still hurt, and confused by all of this, so it took him a little while longer to get use to the fact that they were going to be a family, whether or not he liked the idea of it. Which he didn't.

She leaned over and kissed him on his lips as they pulled into her parents drive way. He slowly pulled away, not trying to make it entirely obvious that he wasn't comfortable with that. She giggled, "I just want to thank you for being here." He nodded emotionlessly, because when he needed her, it was the hardest thing for her to do. Now that she needed him he was there, he didn't even have to think about it, he just went. And maybe that was because she was carrying his child. A love that he would do anything for, you didn't have to ask him twice, because although the face of the child was non-existent, he knew with his heart that he loved it, because it was his own. Confused he wondered why it was so hard for her to do something as easy as that, for someone she loved. Then again, maybe she didn't know what the term love meant.

"You okay?" She asked concerned as to why he didn't speak the whole ride over there.

"Yeah, I'm fine. I'm just a little exhausted, stressed, annoyed. I don't know, it's a lot of things wrapped up into one big ball."

She flashed her hair out of her face and smiled as he spoke with his nostrils flaring in anger. "I hope you feel better after tonight Nate. Really, I do." He looked up at her and admired her beauty. For that instant, he compared her to Casey, Casey was flawless in her appearance, because she gave off that look of pure innocence, and it was believable because she backed it up with her character. Angelique was beautiful, but her flaws were evident. Casey always taught him not to judge a person by their looks because you really don't know them as much as their appearances try to make you think you do. But he was convinced that Angelique's flaws were evident to the world; at least the world around him because, no one else would have gone back to her in his situation, and here he is, by her side.

They were greeted by Angelique's little brother Matthew who was 18. He hugged his sister and gave Nathan his props. "Long time no see Nate, how you been?" Before he got the opportunity to answer,

Angelique interrupted, "Excuse me, lady with a baby here, you should be asking me how I been. Not nice Matt." Nathan and Matthew looked at each other and just shook their heads.

"You ain't never ever gonna change right Angelique? It's always about you, somehow. You're such a bitch." Matt said shutting the front door and walked away from them. Nathan laughed to himself, and Angelique looked back at him because she felt bad that her younger brother said that in front of Nathan, when she was in the process of trying to get him back on her side.

Nathan brushed past her and she spoke, "Nathan don't listen to him, I was just joking."

"He sees what everyone else sees Angelique, face it that's just how you are… you weren't joking, you were living."

She looked in his direction and pouted a little. She pretended as though it did, but it didn't phase her. She knew she was a bitch, like he said, everyone did.

CHAPTER FIFTEEN

I do...or do I?

Pacing and stressing on the treadmill, Nathan and Gregory were in a heated debate over baby names. "I don't even know why we're having this discussion Nate, Quanel is definitely more unique then Joshua man, come on." Nathan looked over at his friend and wiped the sweat from his brow.

"I don't even know why you guys are even having this conversation at all; you all know that Queen B, Angelique is going to name the baby, Mercedes because she's so high maintenance." Steven replied.

Shawn smiled and added, "Or credit card because she has to have one in every colour, now she'll have a black one."

The boys laughed in agreement.

"So how much money have you passed out on this occasion for her?" Shawn asked, very interested in his response.

Nathan hesitated a little, "like, 6 bills." The boys were stunned. "My son deserves the best." Nathan added trying to cover it up; just so that the boys don't think his ridiculous baby mother didn't put him up to it.

"Riiiiiiight!" They said in unison.

After running for about twenty minutes, the boys went onto lifting weights, still conversing about Angelique. "So like does her belly got them stretch marks on it yet Nate man?"

"I don't even look at her belly."

Nathan sighed, "I'm getting really tired of Angelique. Everything isn't about her guys, can we change the topic, for at least one second." Again, the boys laughed because Nathan didn't believe that it wasn't about her all day everyday. It most definitely was. Especially as long as he was with her, it would be about her. After hearing the laughter, he smiled; "Fuck you guys, she's different now."

Gregory commented, "I hope your hopes aren't too high my man." Nathan looked on for him to continue his point.

"You can't change someone especially a head strong individual like Angelique. She may not act right but, she aint stupid, she's manipulative. Just because she said she's changed, or implies she's changed, don't mean shit."

"I use to be in love with this girl, something has to still be there. Or else I wouldn't be here. You can't tell me that I was loving her in vain."

Steven looked at him as if he were joking; "tell me you're not considering being with her forever ever!"

Nathan nodded, "I have to try."

"What about Casey?" Steven argued back.

"What about her Steven? She let me go, remember?"

"Because you fucked her over! She actually loved you man. I'm not gonna sit here and watch you let Angelique take your ass for a ride. This is a game to Angelique, don't you see that. She wins! She's in control; she turns it on and off when she feels the need to. Come on man." He threw his towel down, and in exaggeration Gregory jumped back to dodge the towel from hitting him.

Nathan couldn't believe what he was hearing. He couldn't believe that Steven was getting so emotional about the situation that really didn't affect his life at all. But he genuinely was that kind of person, he hated to see them depressed or doing bad. He liked when they were all on the same page, and Nathan, was a couple chapters behind.

"Take it easy Steven, I'll handle this." Nathan assured him.

"Will you? I don't see you handling nothing! And you're quick to talk about loving Angelique in vain, so isn't that what you'd call your "love" for Casey, in vain Nate? They both can't be real. In every sense of the word." Steven walked away from his group of friends and headed out the front door of the gym with his gym bag in his hand. Shawn and Greg looked over at Nathan who was bewildered at what really just happened. What triggered Steven off in such a manner, to blatantly tell him off over his current circumstances? Steven knew better than anybody what Angelique and Casey were like, so why couldn't Nathan understand that his friend obviously thought he was making the wrong decision.

"Did he over react?" Nathan questioned as they walked to their cars.

"He got all, bitchy ex girlfriend on you, that's what he did." Shawn laughed.

"Maybe Nicole aint giving him none. I get that way sometimes." Gregory added and they all laughed, to excuse the awkwardness.

As he got into his car, Nathan sighed another long and stressful sigh. And to think, his purpose for going to the gym was suppose to be stress free, not stress full. He was more stressed than he had been before he got there. Womp!

To Nathans surprise, he woke up the next morning with the smell of breakfast in the air. Angelique was in the kitchen cooking him breakfast and that was good, because he was in the mood for the omelet and sausage meal, she had prepared for him.

"What's the occasion?"

She hopped on the stool beside him, "I have a doctors appointment today." Nathan laughed as he put a sausage link in his mouth.

"Cool, can you have a doctors appointment everyday? Okay, fine every Friday at least?"

She laughed, "If you want me to cook breakfast, just let me know. I can do that."

Nathan knew there was more to the breakfast shit. She was there for almost three weeks now and that morning she decided to cook breakfast. He didn't even have to say anything, just looking at her intimidated her and she spoke. "I was wondering if you could consider, us getting married, again."

He looked at her like she was joking. She wasn't. He choked on the sausage link and cleared his throat. "And you cooked breakfast, so I'd say yes?"

"No I wanted to show you that I still care about you despite everything. And I'm willing to work hard for us." Nathan didn't want to say yes, but as far as he was concerned, Angelique and that baby, were his priorities.

"I'll think about it. I'll think about us."

She smiled, "Thank you, that's all I ask."

As they drove to the doctors' appointment the Wednesday afternoon, Nathan couldn't help but think about Casey. He was doing this for her, but why did he feel like he was hurting her at the same time? Maybe what Steven said had an impact on his thoughts. Being as he didn't have her cell phone number, he couldn't call her. He called her office Tuesday morning while he was at work but her secretary told him she was on a business trip for the next three weeks, and she couldn't give out her cell phone number, for all her important contacts had it. Disappointed he figured he'd go on living life with Angelique and see how it worked out.

They pulled into the parking lot and walked inside. As they sat and waited for the doctor to come in, Angelique laid back and held her premature belly. As she lay there, Nathan ran his hand through her hair and just gazed into each others eyes. "These past two days have been good, getting to that place in your heart." She wasn't there yet and they both knew that but she hoped he wouldn't shut her down. Same time the doctor walked in and gave them both a smile.

"Hello guys, how are things?" Nathan decided to speak.

"Good. We're anxious to look at the baby."

The doctor smiled, he enjoyed seeing an excited couple who've been blessed with a baby. "Good, that's good to hear Nathan." Nathan nodded and realized what the doctor meant when he said that.

"Yeah, I've had a change of heart. I've been put on a different path."

Doctor Gale nodded and placed the transducer on Angelique's belly. As they watched in amazement, Angelique grabbed for Nathans hand and held onto it tight. Nathan laughed and said, "Wow! Look at our baby, Angel" She smiled and a single tear fell from her eye. "I know it's beautiful." After viewing the ultrasound and having doctor Gale explain to them what was going on, he finished by saying, "Well Angelique, you are exactly 10 weeks pregnant." He looked at his calendar "Well today is, May 21st. So yes, exactly 2 months and 2 weeks pregnant."

Nathan let go of her hand. As the doctor printed out the picture for them Nathan moved away from her. "Doc, you can tell exactly when the baby was conceived?"

"Yes we can. March 10th, 10 weeks ago."

Nathan shook his head and asked him, "Are you sure?"

Doctor Gale was a little perplexed. "Yes Nathan. What's the matter?"

Nathan got really hot and bothered as he spoke, "This baby isn't mine."

Angelique sat up, "What are you talking about? You are the father Nathan."

Nathan tried to laugh it off through all his anger. "You were still in Europe March 10th. I'll be in the car. Excuse me doctor." As he left Angelique looked up at Doctor Gale, swallowed her spit, and then turned her head to the floor.

Nathan walked out of the office and went downstairs to his car. As he waited for her he was going insane! How could he be so stupid? He knew and his friends knew all along that something wasn't right about the surprise pregnancy. He felt foul. How could he have gotten so close to her when she was deceitful the WHOLE TIME?

There were a million and one things running through Nathans mind and he couldn't even begin to think about how he hurt Casey and it was all Angelique's fault. He thought about when his friends were over when Gregory asked her about her birth control pills and it hit him.

He flung open his glove compartment and looked through her make up case that she left in there. And low and behold he found her birth control pills. The last pill she had taken was February 28th the day before she left for Europe.

As he closed up the pills she opened the car door.

"Okay I know what you're thinking Nathan and I can explain."

"Explain to me why you weren't on your pills, why you didn't keep your pills. And WHY YOU HAD SEX WITH SOMEONE ELSE?" He threw the pills in her lap and she shook her head.

"I only slept with you."

"You didn't sleep with me in March Angelique. Matter of fact the last time we slept together was February 28th and as you can tell from your full pack of birth control pills. You were ON IT that night! WOW AND TO THINK, I WAS CONSIDERING MARRYING YOU! You lied to me. You been lying to me for God knows how long. And then you try to cover it up! YOU KNEW THAT BABY WASN'T MINE. AND STILL, BECAUSE YOU WANT THE HOLLYWOOD LIFESTYLE, YOU LIED TO ME, SO YOU COULD LIVE IT."

They pulled into the drive way, "If that's how you want to live GO AHEAD. IT'S LONELY AT THE TOP ANGELIQUE!" and he slammed the car door with her still inside. He stormed up the steps and chucked opened the door and headed straight for the bedroom. He picked up her blackberry and skimmed through her text messages. Michael, Michael, Michael, Michael, Michael, Michael. The messages were pretty much all the same. "Hey Love, I Miss you. Wake up beautiful."

But what caught him off his stance was a text message sent March 11th that read, 'Girl I didn't know you could put it down so nice. Let's meet up tonight, so we could talk about sex...lol again!' He checked her response and she said, 'I'm excited already. I don't even know how many times it's been now, I've lost count. You bring out the freak in me.' Angelique walked in the room as he finished reading the sentence.

Same time, the berry rang and it was Michael, Nathan didn't even hesitate to answer it. "You were fucking my girl?"

Angelique ran over, "Nathan stop it!"

"Get out of my face!"

Michael answered, "Pardon me?"

"You were fucking my girl, you deaf motherfucker. Well come and get her! Pick her up on Young Street, that's where whores belong!"

He ended the call and threw her phone down the hall, destroying the precious berry. She looked at him like, why did you just do that? "Don't you even look at me! You were messing around on me while we were still together Angelique?" She held her head as tears poured out her eyes. "WHY ARE YOU CRYING?"

She still didn't answer. He walked over to the closet and began tearing her clothes off the hangers throwing them into the hall. "What are you doing Nathan?"

"Spring cleaning sweetie, you got to get the hell up out of here!"

"It was a mistake."

"EVERYTHING YOU DO IS A MISTAKE. YOU MISSING THE FUNERAL WAS A MISTAKE. YOU CHEATING ON ME WAS A MISTAKE. YOU COMING HOME WAS A MISTAKE!"

She sat in her pile of clothes that he continued to throw out at her and she quickly got up as he moved onto her shoes. "I'm sorry. You don't know how sorry I am."

"Listen to me; I don't believe a word that comes out of your mouth. You're a liar, a cheater, a user and a bloody disappointment! YOU FUCKED ANOTHER MAN ON THE DAY MY PARENTS WERE FUCKING BURIED! AND ALL YOU CAN SAY IS YOUR SORRY? So tell me when exactly did it happen? In the morning while we were at the church, in the afternoon when were at the burial site, or around 4 o clock when everyone came here for dinner?" She didn't answer. "Do you know how disrespectful that was? I GAVE UP THE BEST GIRL IN THE WORLD FOR YOU! For you! The girl who promised she would no longer disappoint me. The girl who I put over EVERYBODY ELSE, everyone who saw that there was NOTHING right about you. The girl I vowed was an Angel. Well you're not an Angel, YOU'RE THE DAMN DEVIL."

After finishing with her clothes and shoes he walked into the bathroom and started to clear out her feminine products. Tampons, pads, hair scrunchies and three different types of hair irons we're thrown in every direction. She called out for him to stop and he ignored her. "My parents DIED and you want to know why they killed themselves? Because I told them I was marrying YOU!" Nathans mind flashed back to the night at his parents' house and went crazy. "He said and I quote, you let your little Angel come into your life and then you erased us out of it! She doesn't care about you Nathan are you blind, is what he said. And I DEFENDED YOU! I LOST TWO PARENTS AT THE EXPENSE OF YOU! My sister lost her parents; my niece lost her grandparents BECAUSE OF YOU!" Angelique couldn't stop crying, "No, It's not my fault."

"EVERY FAILURE IN MY LIFE IS YOUR FAULT! You brain washed me. Every time you made me think, if all I had was you everything would be okay. I was SELFISH and neglected those who really loved me and now, more than half of them are gone! And still, you cheated on me, after I gave you everything you ever needed, everything you ever wanted. And you...' he broke off. 'You weren't even there for me, you were too busy fucking some other punk, at the expense of my life! Did you even take a minute...no a second to think of what you were doing to me? Oh yeah, your too fucking selfish, all you think about is Angelique."

He walked into the kitchen and grabbed four big garbage bags and filled them with all her things. After filling them he walked over to her drawer on the night table and emptied it in a garbage bag. She ran over to him and he put his hand in her face. "Don't come near me or like the rest of your shit, I will throw you out on the curb." she backed off drowning in her own tears.

"Can I explain?"

Tying up the garbage bags he laughed, "And say what? Yes Nathan I did sleep with Michael. I ALREADY KNOW THAT! THE PROOF IS IN YOUR UTERUS HONEY!" He laughed to himself as a thought popped up in his head. "That's why my dad didn't take the job, isn't it! He KNEW you were fucking around with Michael." He looked at her, "DIDN'T HE?"

She tried to avoid eye contact with him but he wouldn't let her.

"He didn't know, he assumed."

Nathan smirked, "And they say never trust your assumptions because there not facts. But he couldn't be more right about this slut that I wanted to marry." He walked onto the balcony to catch some air before he do something he regrets, like throw her off it. She knew better not to near the balcony door, because she'd never she the other side of it again. He paced back and fourth, inhaling and exhaling heavily, trying to process the mind blowing information that she laid out in front of him. If he hadn't told his dad to stay out of his relationship, that leap year, wouldn't have been such a horrible one to remember.

"I FELT ALONE NATE!" She called from the bedroom.

He walked back in and Nathan stopped and eyed her through the bedroom mirror. "ALONE? YOU DON'T KNOW HOW IT FEELS

TO BE ALONE OBVIOUSLY! I WAS ALONE. And you knew that. And you come back and you claim you love me!"

"I WAS BY MYSELF IN EUROPE AND I MISSED YOU. And I DO LOVE YOU"

"THEN LOVE SHOULDA BROUGHT YOUR ASS HOME! FUUUUUUCK! I can't believe you. You were gone for a mere nine days, and already you missed me. And you felt better by having sex with someone else, after I called you and said, my parents just died, come down here to be with me. After your meeting got cancelled, you said hey Mike lets FUCK?"

After he threw her things down the steps outside. She followed him and spoke just to be heard.

"I fucked up. I know that, but please don't do this, I can't be with him."

"And this just in, you cant and won't ever be with me." She folded her arms and wept. "Were you having sex with him, before we got engaged?" She looked offended at his question.

She nodded, the truth hurt. "But when we got engaged, I said I didn't need him."

"NEED HIM? For what? What, our sexual relations weren't good enough?"

She pulled on her hair, as she saw her life falling apart. "I didn't think you loved me as much as Michael claimed to, but then you proposed and I was sure."

Nathan just stared at her. "After moving heaven and earth for you on several different occasions, you thought I didn't love you. Only a fool would do what I did for you, for someone they didn't care about."

"I have a problem. I don't know why I hurt you."

"How many times did you have sex with him."

She didn't want to answer, but the look in his eyes indicated that she had to. "I can't remember."

"Too many times to remember?"

She nodded.

"You fucking disgust me!"

He walked down into the basement. He grabbed his hammer and headed right back up the stairs. He passed her on the stairs and walked right into the living room. He looked viciously at the 46' flat screen

Samsung T.V that Angelique bought for him as a house warming gift. Within an instant he swung the hammer into the television set and battered it until it fell to the floor.

She covered her mouth and watched him in his anger and all his rage. He threw the hammer at the remains and walked away from it. "I did everything for you Angelique. And all you did for me was buy me this fucking T.V. But that's cool; you'll get what you deserve. Now, get out of my house."

"Where am I supposed to go?" She managed to get out.

Laughing hysterically, "I'm tired of caring about you Angelique, don't you get it? You mean NOTHING to me; the gum on the bottom of my shoe means more to me. The shit that comes out of my ass means more to me than you do. You mean nothing. I don't care about you. Hop in your car and drive to Never land, India, off a cliff. I -DON'T-GIVE-A-FUCK! Just don't drive by here anymore! LOVE DON'T LIVE HERE ANYMORE! Meaning You. I hate you. I hate the way you look, I hate that I met you. I hate EVERYTHING ABOUT YOU, now leave. 2 and a half years of your bullshit, for ONCE do me a favor and leave!"

Nathan just let her have it. His words were eating away at her confidence, her soul, and her mind! "And you see that pretty little Porsche you're driving that I so kindly bought for you, while you were cheating on me? Yeah, I haven't been paying the car payments on it, so know that as soon as you leave here, I will be calling to have it repossessed." Knowing her life was over she walked over to the side door and grabbed her purse and car keys and tried one more time for some mercy.

"Please don't make me go." She stood there pleading.

"Please don't make me call the police and have you dragged out of here."

He stuck out his hand and she put the house key in it. "We agreed to play no games Angelique. And you did. But that's my fault; I have more sense than that. Now get the hell up outta my house!" She tried to walk over to him. "GET OUT!" She clenched back in fear and turned around and walked down the steps. He wanted to hit her, but the man he was, backed off. He closed the door and walked into his room. She loaded the things in her car and sat in the driver seat and cried. After about an hour of crying, she backed out of the drive way and left. Not knowing where she was headed or how to find the pieces of her demolished heart.

Nathan went into his bedroom and immediately tore the sheets off the bed and threw them in the laundry. He was cleaning his house and washing his hands clean of any and everything that reminded him of Angelique Walters. The devil in disguise.

Later on that day, Nathan received a phone call from Steven, maybe he had a feeling shit turned sour, within the 48 hours of them last speaking. He didn't know if he should answer the phone or not, so he let his cell phone ring. After Steven hung up, he called the house phone and the answer machine picked it up. "Nate, I know you're there. Just don't be stupid and pick up the phone. At least understand why I was wilin' out.' Nathan just looked at the machine, as he sat on his bed. "I see your car in the drive way."

Nathan hopped downstairs and opened the door. Steven walked in and nodded, still looking a little miserable from the day before. Nathan wasn't looking too bright either. As Steven walked in, Nathan headed towards the kitchen; "What's up man?" Nathan asked walking away. He wasn't mad at Steven, so to speak, he was just shocked and a little concerned at his behavior.

"Nothing much, I just dropped Nicole and Alexis off at her moms place." Nathan bit into his muffin and nodded. There was an awkward silence and Nathan laughed out loud, this was just too weird. He felt like they were dating and they got into a fight. Steven was his best friend; it was stupid for them to be acting that way with each other. Steven smiled, "I know what you're thinking. And you're right, this is stupid, my wilin out was stupid too."

Nathan sensed something was wrong. "What's up?"

"Nicole was pregnant."

"Oh wow, congrats man." Nathan quickly jumped in not even noticing his tense.

"She lost it the night before I seen ya'll so. It's been a little rough, since that episode, and well, you know the rest. Your verbal bashing was the result of my anger."

Nathan walked over and hugged him; "No sweat Steven. I'm sorry about that."

Steve sighed knowing that he shouldn't say it but he did, "I'm a little relieved about the situation at the same time, because we ain't ready for another baby Nate. Financially yes, but emotionally no way. We have so much love for each other and Alexis already that it's like we'd be pushing it, between work, each other, the baby and Princess Alexis. You know how she gets." Nathan laughed, knowing how arrogant his goddaughter could really be. Steven was at a tough time in his job and so was his wife. Once the focus was off of that issue, then they could work towards this baby. They would just be stressed.

"So we're good?" Steven tried to reassure himself.

"Definitely. That's life, you win some you lose some, you're right and you're wrong. I've just learned the hard way."

Grabbing an apple, Steven looked his friend in his eyes and could read his thoughts.

"She fucked up didn't she?"

"The baby isn't mine. She lied, and pretended this whole time. She knew from the beginning and she planned on using me. And my dad knew about this punk she was with, and tried to warn me. That's why he hated her with a passion."

Steven let go of the apple and fumbled to catch it back before it hit the ground. "Say word?" Nathan nodded. "That's what's up? Did you kill her?"

"Emotionally. Not physically, I'll leave her to God. I trust him."

"Everything happens for a reason Nathan. But you're good? No scars, no cuts, no bruises? Is your heart still in tact?"

Nathan laughed; "Yeah man." Steven and Nathan headed into the living room and Steven took in his destroyed T.V. Looking over at it he commented; "This has Nathan Anthony Walker written all over it."

"I know, what should I call it?"

Steven and Nathan both laughed.

"Call it, The Truth!"

CHAPTER SIXTEEN

Second Chance At Life And Love

Three months later. By the time Casey got back at the beginning of June, Nathan had some business he needed to take care of out of town. He then flew out to Atlanta to be with his sister and her family. It was Eve's birthday in July and he needed time away from his life, so he flew out to Atlanta to be with the only family he knew. Having a one on one conversation with his sister late one night, they touched on Casey. "So, why are you avoiding going back to her?"

"I'm afraid she doesn't want to have nothing to do with me."

"Well if you explain to her the recent events I'm sure she would understand." Nathan tapped his fingers against the kitchen table. "Yeah and I do that to have Angelique show up with something else to spring on me?" Tanya walked over to the fridge and pulled out some chocolate cake saved from Eve's party earlier that week. After cutting herself a slice and shoving a piece of it in her mouth she said, "Well what else can she bring to the table' she laughed, 'you pretty much told her to go kill herself."

"No I didn't." She looked at him like he was out of his mind.

"YES YOU DID! Why didn't you just hand her the hammer after you were finished with it and show her where to aim?"

He shrugged, "Whatever."

He fanned her off and belched. She screwed up her face and slapped him in his shoulder as she walked over to the sink. "Disgusting! Mom would have slapped you in your head."

"Yeah right after she slapped you for slapping me in my shoulder."

Tanya laughed because she knew it was true. "So seriously, I think you should go back home and try to find Casey."

"She hasn't even tried to get a hold of me."

Tanya spoke, "She's trying to do the right thing by you and well, the baby everyone was to believe was yours. Just go and find her Nate!"

"What are you saying I've overstayed my welcome?"

She laughed, "Yes Nathan, yes I am. It's been a month. Get outta my house."

She turned the lights off in the kitchen and pushed her brother up out of his seat. She stopped at the door of her bedroom. "Good night Nate. Think about what I said."

"I will."

She closed her bedroom door and hollered, "No You WON'T!"

He lay down in his bed in the guest bedroom and fell asleep. He dreamed about how perfect life would be with Casey and how disastrous it was with Angelique, when a few months ago, his heart was telling him completely the opposite. He was supposed to experience this perfection with his Angel and any other girl was not the one meant for him. And throughout his dreams he'd often snap back into reality to really wonder, does your true love only ever show up once, or is there more then one. And if they were once your true love and they then change that face, were they your true love to even begin with? Well if Angelique wasn't his true love what was she? She was a piece of the puzzle called life and without her puzzle piece, life or his dreams wouldn't make sense without her.

The next morning when he woke up, Eve was sitting on his bed playing on his laptop. "Hey Uncle Nate. You got mail." She said it in the animated voice and she busted out laughing. He threw the pillow at her and took his laptop out of her grasp. It was from Casey.

Just checking in to see how things are going with you, Angelique and the baby. I haven't seen you in a minute and I got your email address from your office. Victoria told me you were in ATL and I knew you had to be linked to the office somehow, so I tried my luck with the email. August 20th is my last day in the office at my current location. So I just wanted to say goodbye. They unexpectedly moved it from September to August. And I wanted you to know.

Love, Casey.

His niece looked at him as he shot out of his bed. He looked at his I phone for the date. It was August 5th. "You okay Nate?"

"Yeah E-V-E, I just have an emergency I have to get back to."

She giggled, "Casey?"

"No." He lied.

Logging off his laptop, he looked at his desktop background, which was a picture of him and Casey; quickly shutting his laptop he put it away with all the rest of his things. Nathan messaged his office via I phone and had them book a ticket for him, to later fax over to his sisters place. As Nathan packed up his belongings in his suitcase, Tanya walked in and stared at her daughter throwing clothes at her uncle so he could put it in his suitcase. "You moving out?" She joked.

"Yeah, she emailed me, and um, she's leaving next week. I have to go."

Tanya nodded, "Okay, but I just made breakfast, tell me you're staying for that."

Zipping up his suitcase, Nathan agreed to stay, "Well, I guess. My flight isn't until 4 so; I got a few hours to kill.

They walked into the kitchen and Eve, jumped in the chair closest to the hotdogs. Nathan sat beside her and started serving himself some scrambled eggs and then reached for the toast. "Uncle Nate, can you pass the ketchup, please."

"Sure thing, E-V-E."

He handed his niece the ketchup and looked over at his family, devourer the hot meal in front of them. Devon looked up at him and spoke, "You heading out tonight Nate?"

"Actually, this afternoon. 4pm."

Shoving a strawberry in her mouth Eve commented on her Uncles' statement. "You leaving with Casey?"

Nathan laughed, "You read the email didn't you?"

She laughed and nodded hysterically. He looked at her parents and they both started to laugh. "Now Eve we told you to stay out of things that aren't yours, especially when it comes to adults like mommy, your uncle or myself. It could be something important for work and by accident you cold erase it." Devon was an electrician and spoke from experience of Eve messing with important documents.

Tanya joined in with her husband, "That's an invasion of privacy babe, don't do that again please." She nodded and hit her uncle in his belly underneath the table. Nathan laughed and finished his breakfast as he continued small talk with his family.

Leaving to catch his four o'clock flight Nathan hugged his niece, brother in law and sister. Looking at his sister he knew she had a lot to say, but she didn't. Gracefully she just smiled, knowing exactly where her baby brother was headed. As he hopped in his rent-a-car, she called out, "This is your second chance big head, make me proud!" He stuck out his tongue at her, "Second chance at what?"

"Everything."

He smiled and honked as he drove down the street to the airport.

On the plane ride Nathan thought about his life and where it stood. Within 6 months, he lost his mother. He lost his father. He lost Angelique. He lost a baby. He lost Casey. The only thing he walked in with and left with was his job! But as the plane landed, he thought to himself. He wouldn't forget all that he had lost. He would learn and gain from it all. For every mans loss, could internally be the source of his gain.

CHAPTER SEVENTEEN

Give Up

Unexpectedly; Nathan was called into the office August 8th, for some important meeting. The meeting pretty much lasted all day that there was no way that Casey would still be in the office by the time it ended. He just called it a night and decided to go home and make friends with his sheets. After all, ain't nobody else around. He couldn't call the boys over. One, he had no new T.V as yet and it was nearly the middle of the week, they had priorities and bills to pay just like Nathan did. He hated burdening his boys with his mess. He himself needed a Social Worker, someone who had no other choice but to listen to his foolishness.

The next morning Nathan woke up to his alarm clock buzzing like mad. It was 12:00pm. He realized how many times he must of hit snooze because he should have been at work 3 hours ago.

Quickly getting ready Nathan hopped into his BMW and hit the road. There was no way he was going to hop on the highway. Midday madness is what it was and he wouldn't get to work until 3:00 if he chanced it. So he took the city streets. Driving pass the cemetery, something said stop, pull over and say your hellos.

He walked through the cemetery and found his mom and dad. "Well, I didn't bring you guys any flowers this time, or candy dad, sorry.

But I brought you something better. My apologies. I know how much this apology means to you guys. So here it goes. I messed up and I know you hate that you had to be right but you were. And unfortunately I learned the hardest way possible. Losing you both and losing myself in all of it."

Standing strong and holding it together Nathan bent down and read the bible verse off of his parents' tomb stone, 'Children obey your parents in everything for this pleases the Lord.' It was a chosen scripture for whenever Tanya and Nathan misbehaved their mother would say it. It was then he realized how much he should have obeyed his father.

"And when his parents saw him, they were astonished. And his mother said to him, "Son, why have you treated us so? Behold, your father and I have been searching for you in great distress." And he said to them, "Why were you looking for me? Did you not know that I must be in my Father's house?" And they did not understand the saying that he spoke to them. And he went down with them and came to Nazareth and was submissive to them. And his mother treasured up all these things in her heart. And Jesus increased in wisdom and in stature and in favor with God and man."

Nathan looked up and it was Casey, reciting bible scripture, Luke 2:48. "Hi Nathan. Welcome back." He looked at her and there was a guy standing behind her holding onto her shoulders. Nathan looked him dead in his eye and he nodded at Nathan and Nathan took note that she was pregnant. Nathan stretched out his hand to the man standing behind Casey. "Nathan."

"Jared, nice to meet you."

Nathan lied, "Like wise."

It was silent and Casey swayed a little. She had a bad habit of doing that when she was nervous. "You're pregnant."

She laughed, "Yeah, I was just coming to tell your mom that…or show her rather. She said she would pray for me, because she knew how much I wanted to have kids. And what do you know. Here I am."

Nathan was speechless, he didn't know whether he should ask her if she was seeing someone or if the baby was his. "I know what you're thinking. But don't think it Nate. I moved on." Well, that answered his question without her getting into details. And she practically brought the guy there for a definite reason.

"Well, you look happy."

"Yes. I am."

Instant heartburn. "It's Wednesday right?" She nodded. He realized it was a routine for her and he was crowding her space. She spoke, "I just wanted to make a final stop by, because with the company moving, I didn't know how many Wednesdays I could make down here."

Nathan began to feel very uncomfortable. It didn't make any sense to him. She loved him; she said so in her email. She told him to his face. I thought you loved me, was all he wanted to say but he couldn't say it. Especially not in front of Jared. Picking at unhealed wounds wouldn't make the situation any better or any less awkward. He couldn't help but look at how beautifully she glowed. Now she, she was an angel. An angel that God himself created and wrapped up and wrote to Nathan, all my love, God. Except, he broke her, sent her to the lost and found and someone else found her and made her their own.

"How are things?" she asked.

Tell her that things are bad you dummy, his mind egged him on. "There, uhh, there okay." He still couldn't look past the fact that she was pregnant and doing well without him. He was doing terribly. She looked at him and she knew something was wrong with him, she always knew when something was wrong with him.

"How's Angelique?"

Hearing her name added to his insanity. He couldn't have Casey and he didn't want Angelique and still he felt as though Angelique held all the power to his heart and happiness. "Um, I got to head out to the office. I'll leave you alone. Nice meeting you Jared. You look amazing Casey. Congratulations." He hurried off before she could even respond. Nathan literally ran out of the cemetery. When he reached his car, he could see her staring at him. Starting his ignition he soared off the block, not looking back. Heart broken.

Jared stepped back and walked over to the bench. He let Casey do what she came there to do.

Casey squatted down and put down the flowers she had brought in the middle of the two graves. "You raised an amazing son, guys. But he has his priorities in Angelique and her baby. So that would only mean that me and our baby will play second to them and I don't want him to do that to her, or us. So I won't tell him that this baby is his. Save everyone the heartache I guess. Wish you were here to welcome your grandson." She blew a kiss at each grave and stood up.

She walked over to Jared who sat on the bench. "It's funny that you're sitting there."

Jared looked at her, "Why?"

"That's where Nathan and I had our first kiss."

"Ewe! In a cemetery?" He stood up and put his arm around her.

"It doesn't matter where you are, you idiot. It just happened. Of course we realized after that it was kind of weird and we stopped."

Walking out of the cemetery he asked, "So that's daddy Nate?"

She nodded, "Yup, he's the father alright."

"He looks like a good guy. But I think he thinks I'm the father."

She was silent, she sensed that too. And if that made her situation any easier, she had to make him believe that it wasn't his. "I think you should tell him Case."

She shook her head no. "No way. I don't want him to have a part time father. My baby deserves the best. And I don't think any child should have to suffer that kind of relationship, it's unfair to them."

"So you would rather him have no father? I don't know about you, but I preferred part time than no time when we were little. It made me feel like, at least if he didn't care for mom, he cared for us, and never made their differences affect our relationship."

He was right and as her brother went on she listened open heartedly. "I know you hated the relationship we had with dad Case, but he tried, you can't blame a man for trying. And I guarantee you that Nathan would try, if he just knew."

Casey knew he was right and she wanted nothing more than Nathan to be apart of their baby's life, but she just couldn't let him in. "We'll be fine Jared, no worries." He let go of his sister when they got to his car.

"Who's going to help you out? Are you going to be like one of those celebrities and hire nannies to watch him, feed him, bathe him, and grow him while you're at work?"

They got in the car and he didn't even think about starting the engine, his sister needed to hear what he was saying. "I'll figure it out."

"Will you? It doesn't take long for a man to give up on something he wants and just settle for someone or something else that's convenient."

She held her belly and leaned back on the head rest. She felt her brother looking at her for a minute or two before he started his engine. Casey didn't understand why he was fighting so hard for Nathan. He didn't even know him. He didn't know what their relationship was like. Maybe if he did, he would have fought a lot harder. "When you and Joshua broke up Case, you were damaged. And I never thought you'd recover from that. And then you meet Nathan and he has you smiling, going out, laughing, living life and loving again. You didn't even have time for me anymore. In like January, you swore that all guys were the scum of the earth and you'd never find interest in another one, ever again, because why?"

She answered, "All guys are the same. And they still are, kind of."

Pulling into her driveway, he turned toward his baby sister, "Nathan and Joshua are two different people. I know that and you know that. Don't categorize them as the same people. Just think about it."

She hugged him and whispered "I will."

She kissed him on his cheek, "Good now get out of my car, you got me talking all girly about relationships and what not."

She laughed. "Take care of your self and that baby."

"Or what you'll call children's aid?"

He joked back, "Without hesitation. Oh and Case!"

"Yes my brotha!"

Jared laughed, "I can't be your pretend baby daddy. Lets get real, we have the same parents and for crying out loud Case, we look alike."

She laughed, "I didn't notice. And I also didn't realize that you were married and had two kids of your own."

He sighed, "Yeah, guess you'll have to find someone else." He gasped, "How bout the REAL baby daddy?"

She slammed the car door in his face and laughed up her stairs. Jared was right. But she didn't want to give Nathan more than he can handle. Two kids, a fiancé and a baby momma who was deeply in love with him. That was one soap opera, not worth living. It worked out bad for her, Nathan, the kids and even Angelique. Neglect and temptation was all that that would bring.

She listened to her brother and thought about it for the rest of the night as she did her Yoga in her living room. And she concluded, it would be easier to tell him. Because keeping it from him was killing her and killing him and he didn't even know it. This wasn't a normal break up for Casey. A normal break up consisted of her heart bleeding from all the pain suffered and ended with her losing more than she went in with. But Nathan gave her something. He gave her the opportunity to do something she thought was never a possibility. He gave her the chance to reproduce and she was blessed with a baby that before meeting him she was convinced she could never have.

Holding her belly she laid back on her couch, she realized she couldn't tell him. As much as she loved him, she was doing him a favor by just keeping it to herself. "Sorry baby, but it's just you and mommy."

CHAPTER EIGHTEEN

When You Believe

The next morning Nathan had a dream about his dad. The dream went back to the night his parents died and when Nathan was about to walk off in his room his dad called him back. Nathan was waiting for his dad to tell him he was disappointed in him, but he didn't.

"I don't want you to be a punk and give up on your life like I did. There's nothing in life too hard to get through." Nathan was about to speak and his dad continued, "I loved your mother as much as you love Casey. I'm sorry I took your mother from you guys and I'm sorry your child will have to grow up without his grandparents." Nathan laughed out in his dream. "Dad don't apologize, I understand that you had no control over that. Just like I had no control of her baby's life, it isn't even mine." His dad smirked, "Isn't it though?" And just like that, Nathan woke up after hearing something crash to the floor.

It was a picture frame, Nathan seriously thought about not even getting up and leaving it there, but it was a picture of Casey and his mother. It dropped into the box of things that she had dropped off along with the rest of his moms stuff. He picked up the picture, put it back in the frame and placed it back on his night table.

Oddly enough, he decided to go through the box and there was one of his moms' cashmere sweaters in the box that coincidentally he bought for her. He remembered the exact day he gave her the sweater. She tried it on, spun around and said, "Wow, I feel so young, so hip." Tanya laughed at her mom, for she was always an elegant woman, hip was never in her closet.

Nathan noticed a brightly colored wrapping paper in the box. He picked it up and read the front, it read, To My Nathan, Congrats! Recognizing the writing, he knew it was from Casey. He didn't know whether or not he should open it. Maybe now that they were over, it wasn't for him to see. Get real! He opened it. It was a book and the title read, what to expect when you're expecting, Dad.

His heart felt like it skipped one, two, three beats. She wrote the date in the book, May 11th and again, his heart skipped three more beats. He felt like an idiot, but at the same time he felt really good. He started to smile and his heart began to race. For ONCE, things were looking up for him. Nathan sat up and was totally alert about what was going on around him. He couldn't even think straight.

She was pregnant, for him and she would rather go through that alone, than to tell him. Nathan apprehended that Casey was oblivious to the fact that him and Angelique were over for good. Before leaving his house Nathan decided he needed to be calm and he also needed to make a pit stop.

He called his sister and got her at her office. "Tanya Richards, how may I help you?"

Nathan smiled, "You know it's me, why do you do that?"

"Damn, gotta keep it professional Nate, you know that."

Tanya walked around her office with a portable headset on and had her head in a book, with a highlighter in the other. "What can I do for you?"

"Um, when someone is expecting a baby, what would you buy them?"

She wasn't an idiot, "Why is Casey pregnant?" She was good, really good.

"What makes you think that?"

"Well,' she started as she sat down in her seat. 'You don't know any other girls really that you would be so generous to buy something for. And I know it's not Angelique because I know you wouldn't spend another dime on her. So tell me what happened."

Nathan really just wanted to say I AM THE FATHER, but he played around with his sister for a minute. "Well, I stopped at the cemetery yesterday and Casey showed up, with this guy and a baby in her belly."

"That must have been hard on you Nate."

Nathan laughed, "Yes, until I found out this morning that the baby is mine!"

Calmly Tanya responded, "Pardon me? How do you know that?"

He explained to her the book she bought him and she was hysterical. "Congratulations Nate!" She began to tell him what he could buy her and then they ended the conversation. "Good luck Nate. Today I can honestly say I'm proud to be your sister."

Nathan laughed, "And you couldn't any other day because?"

"Well because, it was Angelique you got pregnant."

He smiled to himself. "Too soon for jokes?" she asked.

He laughed, "Yes."

CHAPTER NINETEEN

Lies & Secrets

"Hey Tracy, is Casey in right now?"

"She actually just stepped out, she should be back in twenty minutes, or so."

He smiled, "that's cool I'll wait. Do me a favor?"

Tracy looked up at him and the baby basket and smiled, "Don't worry I won't tell her. I'm glad your back Nate."

He smiled, "As am I."

He walked pass Tracy with a basket filled with baby soaps, lotions, sleepers, socks, hats, rags, rattles and bottles. He also bought her a dozen roses. Idea courtesy of himself, Tanya suggested the basket, but the flowers were from him and his heart.

They both screamed with joy and excitement. His sister assured him that he should convince her to leave the man she was with to be with him, and have them start their own family. Nathan vowed if he was going to do anything to change his life and make good, he would most definitely do that.

He walked into her office and smelt the scents of her hair, her clothes and her heavenly body. Placing the basket in the middle of her desk, he heard her heels clicking down the hall and was certain it was her. After hearing her jolly laugh a rush of anxiety took over his body. Nathan ran to the door and hid behind it.

Casey walked into her office with her head in some papers. She closed the door without lifting her head up and at the corner of her eye, she noticed she basket of goodies on her desk. She put the papers down beside the basket and called out, "Tracy, who's this from?"

Nathan moved from the door, "Me."

Scaring her she turned and pushed back her Prada glasses to the brim of her nose. "I got the book."

"Shit."

"What do you mean by that?"

"I forgot I even did that. I guess I was so wrapped up in us that I forgot I bought that and dropped it in that box, before I dropped it off by your place."

He looked confused. "You weren't going to tell me, ever?"

She sat on the edge of her desk, "No. I didn't want to interfere with your relationship with Angelique."

"There is no relationship Casey. We're done."

She stood up, "Why? Because of me and our son? No Nathan! You can't do that I won't let you do that!"

"Stop being so sympathetic to other people Casey. Think about yourself for once, please. We stopped talking since you went on your business trip. She cheated on me. She had been cheating on me from before my parents even died. And I found out." He was still hurt, she could tell in his voice.

Casey had nothing but regret in her eyes, she walked over to him and raised her left hand to his cheek and rubbed his face. "I'm sorry, I should have warned you."

He pulled away, "Warned me?"

Casey caught her self and turned her back, "I had a feeling that their was someone else in her life, when I met her."

"Why, was someone there? What was it?"

She didn't want to say anything to him because it didn't even matter after that. "Someone called her and she said hi baby. But uhh, I was convinced it was you."

He looked at her, "But..."

"But I called you right after and you answered."

Something came to him, "And that's why you asked me if I talked to Angelique that day?" She nodded. "Do you know that if you had just told me all of that Casey, we wouldn't have to of been apart for so long."

She felt insulted. "Yeah well if you had just told me that you were engaged and living a secret other life than this criminal lawyer, from the beginning I would of just left you alone. And I wouldn't even have heard that conversation."

"You saying you wish you never met me?"

She shouted "I'm saying I wish you never lied to me!"

"I didn't lie to you Casey!"

"You withheld the truth Nathan, you might as well call it a lie!"

"You mean the same truth you withheld from me?"

She folded her arms and Tracy walked in, interrupting the tension they held in the room. "Hey Casey, sorry to intrude but Ms. Kelly is here to see you."

"Thank you Tracy, I'll be right out to welcome her."

She looked at Nathan who just looked to the sky. He knew the conversation had to be ended and he didn't want it to be that way. He started to turn to leave, knowing that she had work to get back to. "Wait, so the baby isn't yours?"

"Not a chance in hell."

Looking back to Casey feeling relieved that she stopped him from leaving, he walked over and touched her stomach. She put her hand on top of his as the baby moved within his mothers' womb. It felt so perfect. Nathan raised his head and looked at Casey who was falling in love with him all over again at that very moment "I never told you what happened the night my parents died."

"You don't have to." She assured him, knowing how much pain it brought to him, even remembering that tragic night.

"No, I want to. My dad felt like I erased them out of my life to include Angelique. I let her take advantage of me and she didn't care about me and I was blind to the truth. He was upset because of my relationship with Angelique." Nathan laughed, "I'm starting to think that that's the reason why he suffered from such an illness. The argument was about Angelique, their death was because of Angelique, and then there's you." She began to tear up. "My life is with you. My life only makes sense with you. My life was right with you. They want me to be happy with you!" She closed her eyes. "Tell me that you don't feel for him the way you do for me."

"Him? Him who?"

"The guy you moved on with. You know at the cemetery"

She laughed, knowing that she shouldn't. "There is no guy Nathan, Jared's my brother. When I said I moved on I meant alone."

He squeezed her hands relieved and spoke really softly, "Look I love you Casey Green and I need you. Please." He looked in her eyes as the effects of her tears sparkled in the sunlight.

"I'm afraid. I'm afraid to love you as much as I do, because I don't want to be hurt. Love hates us Nate."

"You know I won't hurt you Casey, Never. You have my word. No more lies, no more secrets. Just love me. Trust our love. And I'll take care of you and him and us."

She nodded and hugged him. Tears ran down her cheek and she whispered, "I knew you'd say that."

The next week Casey brought some stuff over to Nathans house to initiate her move in. They decided if they were going to make things work and be a happy family they would start by living together. Nathan had the boys over and Gregory opened the door, "Who's this pretty lady in front of me?"

She laughed, "Help me with one of these boxes and I'll tell you my name."

He quickly grabbed the box out of her hand, and she pulled in her luggage. "I'm Casey by the way." Putting the box down in the living room he kissed her hand.

"Pleasure to meet you, I'm Gregory. And for the record, you're prettier than Angelique!" She laughed out loud and Nathan heard her and he rushed out of the spare room, closing the door behind him.

"Hey babe." He kissed her, "I didn't know you were stopping by."

He slapped Gregory in the back of his head for not warning him. "I got an early lunch babe, so I stopped by my place and brought some things, that I could manage of course."

"You know you shouldn't be holding heavy objects."

"Nate, I'm good. They weren't that heavy. You took all the heavy boxes last night remember?"

Shawn and Steven walked out of the spare room and joined the circle of conversation. Steven hugged her, "Hey beautiful how you doing?"

"I'm good, how's Nicole."

"Great, great." Steven answered.

"Well I guess I'm the only stranger in the room." The boys laughed as Shawn squeezed his way in to face Casey.

"Shawn. Shawn Edwards." He shook her hand.

"Nice to meet you Shawn, Casey."

" Oh no girl, you don't have to introduce yourself, we know alllllllllllllllllllll about you."

Steven slapped him in his head back and Nathan spoke, "Thanks."

Steven nodded. "Anytime."

"Well I hope it's all good."

The boys answered, "Oh Yeahhhh."

Through her laugh Casey was definitely still worried. The boys made her feel welcomed and as Nathan held onto her while the boys started small conversation, it was a good feeling to be around them. "What time do you have to get back to the office Case?" Nathan asked her as she sat down on the couch.

"Well, I actually have some more stuff in the car, and I have a 12:30 appointment. So as soon as you and your muscles bring those in, I can head out."

The boys took the hint, "We'll take care of that."

Steven said and pulled Shawn by his shirt collar. Nathan joined them and stopped at the living room door, "Greg you coming or what?"

"Yeah in a sec, I just want to say something to Casey right quick."

He motioned him choking Greg if he said something stupid and showed him that he was watching. Gregory laughed and said, "Just go outside." As Casey sat in her yellow and green summer dress, with a bright yellow flower stuck in her curls he smiled, "It's good to finally meet you. It is my pleasure to welcome you to the family."

Smiling back, Casey spoke, "Thank you. I heard about the family once before. So I'm anxious to see what you guys are about."

She looked a little tense and as Gregory got up he commented, "I want to apologize for what Angelique did to you and Nathan. We all saw that she was no good, and um, let's just say Nathan was the last one to see it for himself. She had a hold on him and we were all really surprised when he opened up his life to someone else."

"Don't apologize. It wasn't your fault."

He nodded, "Well, still. We saw how happy he was with you, so. I apologize on her behalf. She almost ruined a good thing."

Casey laughed and leaned back in the chair. "Yeah well, no one can destroy what was meant to be. Right?"

Gregory laughed and walked out, "Amen!"

As the boys finished bringing in Casey's belongings, she watched from the steps with a glass of water in her hand. "Thank you boys." They all uttered their no problems and went inside as Nathan and Casey stood on the steps alone. "Well babe, I should head back. I don't want to miss this important meeting."

"What's this so important meeting about?"

Casey held his hands and swung them in and out, "Yeah, wouldn't you like to know."

Nathan didn't even remember that her company was moving that weekend. But Casey had set up a meeting to come to terms with her relocating the company.

"So when should I expect you back home?"

"Um, I don't know. Don't count on it being anytime soon though. So you and the boys can, party hard until I get back home."

They laughed, because in a strange way they both liked the way that sounded. They were going to be together and it felt good for them to be close and not apart. "Oh yeah, at 6 I have a fitting for Jacqueline's wedding, remember? So I'm just going to stay at the office until then. Cool?"

"Cool babe. Oh and speaking about fitting. I realize those clothes you use to be able to fit in, won't be fitting you anymore. So, I had Victoria from the office pick up a gift certificate for you, for all your maternity clothes needs."

Casey loved shopping and shopping always made her happy, even if it was for clothes three sizes bigger than she was use to wearing. She couldn't even speak to thank him, he hugged Casey and she rushed off to take care of business. "Love you Nate. " She called as she started the engine.

Walking back inside, Nathan took a deep breath. "Home sweet home!"

Chapter Twenty

Walk Away

After brushing his teeth the next day, Nathan heard a knock at his front door. He walked over to the door and opened it for none other than Angelique. If looks could kill, she would have curled up and died, on the spot! "What's wrong with your face?" He asked looking at the black and blue welt on the left side of her face.

"I had an accident last night."

Nathan laughed, "With what? Someone's fist?" She looked away and he paused, "He hit you didn't he?"

She felt like a fool to admit it, but she had no other choice. "Yeah, he did."

"What did you do?" Nathan folded his arms to get the inside scoop, he needed a juicy story, his life was overrated.

She looked at him disgusted that he wanted to know details. "I talked to his wife about our relationship. And she threatened to leave him."

Nathan laughed his heart out. "WOW! You never learn do you, always somehow gotta be about you, the home wrecker. Weren't you the least bit ashamed that you were sleeping with a married man? A father? You had to take the "necessary" steps to break up his marriage, so you could be happy. And now look at you." He continued to laugh and she just looked to the floor.

"Sooooo, what do you want?"

She was shocked by his response. "Wow."

"What did you come here looking for a shoulder to cry on? Some sympathy? Somebody to care maybe?"

"No, I miss you Nate."

He rested his head on the side of the door and laughed. "I wish I could say I felt the same. But I would be lying to you. And I don't lie to the ones I care about. But in your case, once cared about."

"AHHHHHHHHHHHHHHHHHHHHHHH!"

He heard Casey scream out. "Baby, Baby, Baby!" She ran from the bedroom. "The baby just kicked!"

"Oh my God!" Nathan exclaimed, he hugged her and she kissed him.

Casey noticed Angelique at the door and smiled, "Hi Angelique, nice seeing you again." Casey gave her a dirty look and skipped off into the kitchen screaming out in happiness.

"Is that the best girl in the world you lost because of me? She lives here now?" Angelique remembered when he barked that at her, the day he found out she cheated on him.

As nonchalantly as he could, he said, "Yes. And yes."

Tears came to her eyes. "How far along is she?"

"4 months. Anymore questions officer?"

"I just find it weird that you got another girl pregnant and you give me so much shit for what I did."

Nathan stood up straight and ignored the fact that she was now crying! "What you and I did is nowhere related, okay? You were having an affair while you and I were still engaged! After our engagement was off, which you initiated by giving me back my ring, I pursued a relationship with a woman, not girl. A woman, who was there for me, when my fiancé was too busy handling some other mans sexual needs. And I don't think you're in any position to stand there trying to flip the script on me. We're done Angelique. I love her. She is my life; you were a bad habit that she taught me how to quit. Now please just be gone."

Holding her belly and basically acting like a poor little thing, she held back her tears to the best of her abilities. "You're a great man Nate. I just wish I didn't take advantage of that, and valued what I had when

I had it." It was too late for that. He wanted to be an ass and shut his door but he didn't.

"Come here."

She walked over to him and he hugged her. "My fiancé is a Social Worker, I'm sure she'd be willing to help you out. But I can't, this can never happen. I don't want to pursue, any kind of a relationship with you." He reached over to his wallet on the side table and handed her Casey's card.

Teary eyed, she understood where he was coming from, "I'm sorry about your mom and your dad Nathan. I'm sorry they had to be right about me. I hope one day when you don't blame me anymore, you can take me down to the cemetery so I can pay my respects, because I truly am hurting, especially because you're right, and they were right too."

Nathan didn't know what to say exactly, he just felt bad for her. Actually wanted to yell and ask her what took her so long, but clearly her and her face had been through enough.

"Take care of yourself. And that baby."

"You too."

She walked down the steps and Nathan realized that she had a new car, "Nice car." She laughed and drove off. He shut the door,

"Fiancé? Who's that?" Casey asked hugging him.

"Well, that's if you'll have me."

Casey squeezed him. "You don't even have to ask!" She kissed him. "I'm proud of you, even though you volunteered me to help her. I still love you."

He smiled, "Good, you don't have to love her. Shoot, you don't even have to like her. But you've done so much with me, I know you can do something with that." He looked at her and had a weird look on his face, expressing how extreme Angelique would be. "Big Money." He joked.

She laughed and rested her head on his chest and screamed out, "We're getting MARRIED!" He laughed.

"Babe, I made some tea, can you bring the tray for me please?" Nathan nodded and watched as Casey walked off. She held onto her belly and said, "Mommy's proud of daddy. Yes she is, very very proud of daddy!"

They sat in the bed together and Casey rubbed her belly. "What are you thinking about?" Nathan asked her.

"I'm thinking about miracles, and how fortunate I've been this year with you and this baby."

Nathan leaned back on his pillows and sighed. "You know, I don't want to sound like an ass, but if my parents hadn't died. I don't know if I'd ever meet you." She rolled on her side and looked up at him.

"You don't sound like an ass."

"If it wasn't for you, I'd did be this stuck up rich boy, working them hours to pay for Angelique's baby. As a fool, I would have probably stayed with her if the situation remained the way it is now."

She rose to her elbow, "We were meant to be together Nate, I feel it. I feel it right here." She said putting his hand on her belly. "If we didn't meet this way, we would have met another way. Trust that."

"I trust that we were meant to be together and that we are truly one in a million." She looked into his eyes and he spoke, "You're beautiful."

She laughed, "We're beautiful babe." She jumped up and said, "I brought something for you." She ran into his closet and pulled out the collage from her house.

Nathan laughed and said "Wow, that's the best present you could give me, besides you and the baby of course."

She leaned the collage up against his dresser and kissed him as he approached her. "Well that's not all." He sat on the bed. "I made a negotiation meeting last night with Colleen Dixon, my partner at work and, well, she decided to move, so I don't have to."

He got up and grabbed hold of his woman and passionately kissed her for as long as he could until she pulled away and spoke, "So what do you have for me?" She joked with him.

"Well my lady lover, while you were at work for the past two days, the boys and I had a little summin summin, we prepared for you."

She got excited, "Show me!"

"Okay, but you're gonna have to close your eyes."

Casey did as she was told, and he led her down the hall, into the spare room. As she opened her eyes he said, "Thanks for working late these past two days." It was baby blue with white cloud borders. In the right corner was the baby change table, in the middle was his crib and in the left corner, was a cushioned rocking chair, a mini book shelf with baby books, a blue and white tall lamp and a white mini shelf with blue woven baskets with diapers in some and baby toys in the others. In the middle of the wall was a blue and white cross that said, "Bless this baby boy" as well as blue and white baby wall stickers. The crib was complete with little blue and white pillows with the matching plaid quilt and sheets.

Casey wanted to, but her mouth couldn't manage to say wow. "I love it." She smiled and laughed, "I Love It!!!" He hugged her from behind and kissed her head.

"I'm glad."

Just taking it all in Casey felt like a million dollars, the luckiest girl in the entire world.

"Nathaniel."

"Pardon?" She turned to face him.

"That's his name. Nathaniel Jeffery. Walker."

He picked up his fiancé and cradled her in his arms like a baby. "Do you like it?"

He stared in her eyes, "I love it, I love you."

CHAPTER TWENTY ONE

Amazing Grace

After breakfast, Casey decided to take a nap and Nathan decided to take one with his wife to be. Laying on her side, Nathan looked over at his fiancé fast asleep and rubbed her exposed belly as she snoozed peacefully. He kissed her belly and then her. Thinking about the little boy she was carrying he just stared at the little belly in front of her.

Finally he was at peace, at ease, with himself, his life and his parents' death. It was like he could feel his mom and dad just smiling down on him. At that moment he realized, it wasn't his fault. He felt good. He found the love of his life for real and now they would spend eternity together and it felt amazing. Looking at the belly where his unborn son laid, he spoke quietly. "This is for you dad."

He knew he was forgiven and he knew things would start looking up for him and Nathan vowed never to look back. Everything you were, transforms you into what you are. Why look back when the future and all that you are lays on a path ahead of you? And just like that Nathan realized what he was missing. *Something Special.* Or someone made especially for him. *Amazing Grace, how sweet the sound, that saved a wretch like me. I once was lost, but now am found, was blind but now, I see.*

End.

Shoutouts!!

Something Special Thanks

This is a little something special for all my fans! *(Pun Intended)*

First, this thing I occasionally refer to as talent, wouldn't be at all possible without the mindset I obtained from JC himself. You've given me a gift that many throw away or ignore, but you've given me the understanding to use this talent as an advantage to reach out to young minds. And I thank you. And I'm truly grateful for you.

Second those artists, who write the lyrics I live off of. Be it Alicia Keys, Anthony Hamilton, Trey Songs, Jagged Edge or even Dru Hill. I feel like you read my mind, and I want to represent your words and the bond it has with my words and create magic through the stories I write.

Third, the inspirations of my lifetime, from about 2000-2008. My life is what motivates me to write to all of you. The heartache and the emotions and all the feelings are feelings that have occurred in my life once or twice or too many times. The heart of my story springs from the heart of the writer. And I guess, if it wasn't for those heartbreakers or overpowering individuals, what I write wouldn't be real enough.

Omar Tyree. Love your work and I could never think I could do this if it wasn't for you and the novels you write. You among others have inspired the work of yours truly.

My momma dukes and daddy dukes. Pushing me to be more than average, to be better than I believed I was. And for SPOILING me to a certain extent that I knew the difference between rights and privileges. And most importantly knowing that all good comes within time, not money! And all is possible with God. Love you both!

My older siblings, (who would beat me down if they weren't mentioned)

Nats- For introducing me to all the classic novels you read. I wouldn't have taken up reading if you didn't keep me posted with the must reads. Yes for many years I looked up to and wanted to be just like you, and I realized shortly after that I couldn't be you, I was my own person, my mind and heart was headed elsewhere. But you believed in me and always gave me constructive criticism, despite our age difference you respected my ideas and 'bigged dem up!' x o x o

Jamaal- For always listening to me go on and on about how wicked I thought this book was going to be. Although you've yet to diss it's romance and all the emotions. You would always tell me if it sucked! And that's good because, I hate negativity, but you taught me how to be tough and except it and life for what it is. X o x o

Kevin- When I told you I wanted to publish a book when I was 15, you went as far as helping me pick out a title. And didn't trash my ideas, truthfully, I think its because you knew they were good ideas, that I was very passionate about. But always having my back no matter how bratty I got, and even if I didn't deserve you too. You would be there.... if you ever answered your phone ;) X o x o

Shainey Boy & Tasha- Since I met you two, you ALWAYS had nothing more than faith in me, you knew I could do it and you knew how much doing this meant to me. Your faith has brought me this far, and I owe you for giving a damn, and believing that I could do this. X o x o

MY DEAREST FRIENDS From Elementary to High School

They all know who they are. Ones who ever read one of my stories. Ones who have ever had to sit through my mini chapter books like 'Tryna Get Back' or 'Crushed'. All of you who read my 'Intimacies of a Lovers Touch' on face book! Even the ones who would ask me to write them a poem or story for one of their classes, just because they knew writing was my thing. If it wasn't for your feedback I probably would think, my writing sucked and give up on it. Your feedback has been critical to my development. This is for ya'll! Also, I owe it to many of your lives , problems and successes. I reflect on those situations and turn them into my own. Thanks for trusting me with your LIFE! =) If you think anything I write is about you in the slightest sense...it probably is.

Samantha, my little sister- The lil heffer who always had my back! (Wink) She always believed in my stories, my poems, hell even my DREAMS! They always excited her and it made me proud to see how much my writing could effect someone as much as it effected her. When she read a chapter and she said, that's so true. Or that makes sense, I was like EWW, you're lying. But she was serious. In the littlest way in impacted her life and, it felt good. So without her warm encouragements and demands to hurry up and send her something else to read. I would still be on chapter one! X o x o

Tashauna, My LOVE- On msn I could be talking to this girl about, nothing even related to my writing material. And she was still so impressed that she said and I quote. 'Jalesaaaa, please don't ever stop writing. Whatever you do!' I was caught off guard and thought, wth? But I had this girl at the end of her seat…all the time, and her energy, gave me energy to pull off a 21 chapter book. After all Shauna, 21 is the lucky number right? Thanks X o x o

Dee & Roushane- My late night msn crew. Typical girls, striving for more drama, more fights, and most importantly more SEX! I brought my ideas to them and they were all for it. Anticipating the finish of the novel, they egged on this side career I envisioned and drooled as they scrolled down on the Microsoft word document. (LOL) X o x o

Nessa B- No other girl in the world as positive as her. She sees the good never the bad and always commented on my work. Very truthful and soft spoken. The girl whose there when it seems as if no one else is, or ever was. Thanks for understanding me and my creative style of writing Ness. ANDDD my jokes, they were funny and you know it! X o x o

Andre M- For listening to this emotion filled girl rant on about love, heartbreak and a new idea for this book she was writing that remain untitled until further notice =) Although he gave me faulty plots for this story, he did it with a great heart. Trust me when I say no other guy would have sat there and listened to me go on and on about love and kissing. No matter how old I get, some boys are just not that mature! =) x o x o

Mr McCuaig, my grade 12 writers craft teacher, who taught me that any thing you say can be turned into an amazing story. You just have to know how to incorporate the interest, and you have yourself a story.

My Dearest Lauren, Petuli & Diana. - Always believing in Jalesa Wallace For EVERYTHING. You ALWAYS believed in me even when I felt you shouldn't. Helping me along my high school years and pushing me to University to do nothing but good! I LOVE YOU GUYS! MUAHHHHH

And a final thanks to all the ANGELIQUES, NATHANS & CASEYS out there. Or maybe each and every one of those characters live in all of us. The bitch, the liar, the lover, the heartbreaker, the emotional one, the one who cares too much about other people, the selfish one, the pretty one, the one with the pretty smile, the hurt one, the deceived one. The forgiving one. We're not all perfect, and each of us are an Angelique at one time or another, just like we are a Nathan and a Casey. Sometimes we need people to paint a picture or write a book, to see how we ourselves truly are!

Lots of Love Jalesa Wallace